T0063976

# THE HIGH BEAMS MURDER CASE

Volume 6: Zen and the Art of Investigation

Anthony Wolff

authorHOUSE®

*AuthorHouse™ LLC*
*1663 Liberty Drive*
*Bloomington, IN 47403*
*www.authorhouse.com*
*Phone: 1-800-839-8640*



*Published by AuthorHouse 02/20/2014*

*ISBN: 978-1-4918-6655-9 (sc)*
*ISBN: 978-1-4918-6656-6 (e)*



*This book is printed on acid-free paper.*

# PREFACE

## WHO ARE THESE DETECTIVES ANYWAY?

"The eye cannot see itself" an old Zen adage informs us. The Private I's in these case files count on the truth of that statement. People may be self-concerned, but they are rarely self-aware.

In courts of law, guilt or innocence often depends upon its presentation. Juries do not - indeed, they may not - investigate any evidence in order to test its veracity. No, they are obliged to evaluate only what they are shown. Private Investigators, on the other hand, are obliged to look beneath surfaces and to prove to their satisfaction - not the court's - whether or not what appears to be true is actually true. The Private I must have a penetrating eye.

Intuition is a spiritual gift and this, no doubt, is why Wagner & Tilson, Private Investigators does its work so well.

At first glance the little group of P.I.s who solve these often baffling cases seem different from what we (having become familiar with video Dicks) consider "sleuths." They have no oddball sidekicks. They are not alcoholics. They get along well with cops.

George Wagner is the only one who was trained for the job. He obtained a degree in criminology from Temple University in Philadelphia and did exemplary work as an investigator with the Philadelphia Police. These were his golden years. He skied; he danced; he played tennis; he had a Porsche, a Labrador retriever, and a small sailboat. He got married and had a wife, two toddlers, and a house. He was handsome and well built, and he had great hair.

And then one night, in 1999, he and his partner walked into an ambush. His partner was killed and George was shot in the left knee and in his right shoulder's brachial plexus. The pain resulting from his injuries and the twenty-two surgeries he endured throughout the year that followed, left him addicted to a nearly constant morphine drip. By the time he was admitted to a rehab center in Southern California for treatment of his morphine addiction and for physical therapy, he had lost everything previously mentioned except his house, his handsome face, and his great hair.

His wife, tired of visiting a semi-conscious man, divorced him and married a man who had more than enough money to make child support payments unnecessary and, since he was the jealous type, undesirable. They moved far away, and despite the calls George placed and the money and gifts he sent, they soon tended to regard him as non-existent. His wife did have an orchid collection which she boarded with a plant nursery, paying for the plants' care until he was able to accept them. He gave his brother his car, his tennis racquets, his skis, and his sailboat.

At the age of thirty-four he was officially disabled, his right arm and hand had begun to wither slightly from limited use, a frequent result of a severe injury to that nerve center. His knee, too, was troublesome. He could not hold it in a bent position for an extended period of time; and when the weather was bad or he had been standing for too long, he limped a little.

George gave considerable thought to the "disease" of romantic love and decided that he had acquired an immunity to it. He would never again be vulnerable to its delirium. He did not realize that the gods of love regard such pronouncements as hubris of the worst kind and, as such, never allow it to go unpunished. George learned this lesson while working on the case, The Monja Blanca. A sweet girl, half his age and nearly half his weight, would fell him, as he put it, "as young David slew the big dumb Goliath." He understood that while he had no future with her, his future would be filled with her for as long as he had a mind that could think. She had been the victim of the most vicious swindlers he had ever encountered. They had successfully fled the country, but not the range of George's determination to apprehend them. These were master criminals, four of them, and he secretly vowed that he would make them fall, one by one. This was a serious quest. There was nothing quixotic about George Roberts Wagner.

While he was in the hospital receiving treatment for those fateful gunshot wounds, he met Beryl Tilson.

Beryl, a widow whose son Jack was then eleven years old, was working her way through college as a nurse' s aid when she tended George. She had met him previously when he delivered a lecture on the curious differences between aggravated assault and attempted murder, a not uninteresting topic. During the year she tended him, they became friendly enough for him to communicate with her during the year he was in rehab. When he returned to Philadelphia, she picked him up at the airport, drove him home - to a house he had not been inside for two years - and helped him to get settled into a routine with the house and the botanical spoils of his divorce.

After receiving her degree in the Liberal Arts, Beryl tried to find a job with hours that would permit her to be home when her son came home from school each day. Her quest was daunting. Not only was a degree in Liberal Arts regarded as a 'negative' when considering an applicant's qualifications, (the choice of study having demonstrated a lack of foresight for eventual entry into the commercial job market) but by stipulating that she needed to be home no later than 3:30 p.m. each day, she further discouraged personnel managers from putting out their company's welcome mat. The supply of available jobs was somewhat limited.

Beryl, a Zen Buddhist and karate practitioner, was still doing part-time work when George proposed that they open a private investigation agency. Originally he had thought she would function as a "girl Friday" office manager; but when he witnessed her abilities in the martial arts, which, at that time, far exceeded his, he agreed that she should function as a 50-50 partner in the agency, and he helped her through the licensing procedure. She quickly became an excellent marksman on the gun range.

As a Christmas gift he gave her a Beretta to use alternately with her Colt semi-automatic.

The Zen temple she attended was located on Germantown Avenue in a two storey, storefront row of small businesses. Wagner & Tilson, Private Investigators needed a home. Beryl noticed that a building in the same row was advertised for sale. She told George who liked it, bought it, and let Beryl and her son move into the second floor as their residence. Problem solved.

While George considered himself a man's man, Beryl did not see herself as a woman's woman. She had no female friends her own age. None. Acquaintances, yes. She enjoyed warm relationships with a few older women. But Beryl, it surprised her to realize, was a man's woman. She liked men, their freedom to move, to create, to discover, and that inexplicable wildness that came with their physical presence and strength. All of her senses found them agreeable; but she had no desire to domesticate one. Going to sleep with one was nice. But waking up with one of them in her bed? No. No. No. Dawn had an alchemical effect on her sensibilities. "Colors seen by candlelight do not look the same by day," said Elizabeth Barrett Browning, to which Beryl replied, "Amen."

She would find no occasion to alter her orisons until, in the course of solving a missing person's case that involved sexual slavery in a South American rainforest, a case called Skyspirit, she met the Surinamese Southern District's chief criminal investigator. Dawn became conducive to romance. But, as we all know, the odds are always against the success of long distance love affairs. To be stuck in one continent and love a man who is stuck in another holds as much promise for high romance as falling in love with Dorian Gray. In her professional life, she was tough but fair. In matters of lethality, she preferred dim mak points to bullets, the latter being awfully messy.

Perhaps the most unusual of the three detectives is Sensei Percy Wong. The reader may find it useful to know a bit more about his background.

Sensei, Beryl's karate master, left his dojo to go to Taiwan to become a fully ordained Zen Buddhist priest in the Ummon or Yun Men lineage in which he was given the Dharma name Shi Yao Feng. After studying advanced martial arts in both Taiwan and China, he returned to the U.S. to teach karate again and to open a small Zen Buddhist temple - the temple that was down the street from the office Wagner & Tilson would eventually open.

Sensei was quickly considered a great martial arts' master not because, as he explains, "I am good at karate, but because I am better at advertising it." He was of Chinese descent and had been ordained in China, and since China's Chan Buddhism and Gung Fu stand in polite rivalry to Japan's Zen Buddhism and Karate, it was most peculiar to find a priest in China's Yun Men lineage who followed the Japanese Zen liturgy and the martial arts discipline of Karate.

It was only natural that Sensei Percy Wong's Japanese associates proclaimed that his preferences were based on merit, and in fairness to them, he did not care to disabuse them of this notion. In truth, it was Sensei's childhood rebellion against his tyrannical faux-Confucian father that caused him to gravitate to the Japanese forms. Though both of his parents had emigrated from China, his father decried western civilization even as he grew rich exploiting its freedoms and commercial opportunities. With draconian finesse he imposed upon his family the cultural values of the country from which he had fled for his life. He seriously believed that while the rest of the world's population might have come out of Africa, Chinese men came out of heaven. He did not know or care where Chinese women originated so long as they kept their proper place as slaves.

His mother, however, marveled at American diversity and refused to speak Chinese to her children, believing, as she did, in the old fashioned idea that it is wise to speak the language of the country in which one claims citizenship.

At every turn the dear lady outsmarted her obsessively sinophilic husband. Forced to serve rice at every meal along with other mysterious creatures obtained in Cantonese Chinatown, she purchased two Shar Peis that, being from Macau, were given free rein of the dining room. These dogs, despite their pre-Qin dynasty lineage, lacked a discerning palate and proved to be gluttons for bowls of fluffy white stuff. When her husband retreated to his rooms, she served omelettes and Cheerios, milk instead of tea, and at dinner, when he was not there at all, spaghetti instead of chow mein. The family home was crammed with gaudy enameled furniture and torturously carved teak; but on top of the lion-head-ball-claw-legged coffee table, she always placed a book which illustrated the elegant simplicity of such furniture designers as Marcel Breuer; Eileen Gray; Charles Eames; and American Shakers. Sensei adored her; and loved to hear her relate how, when his father ordered her to give their firstborn son a Chinese name; she secretly asked the clerk to record indelibly the name "Percy" which she mistakenly thought was a very American name. To Sensei, if she had named him Abraham Lincoln Wong, she could not have given him a more Yankee handle.

Preferring the cuisines of Italy and Mexico, Sensei avoided Chinese food and prided himself on not knowing a word of Chinese. He balanced this ignorance by an inability to understand Japanese and, because of its inaccessibility, he did not eat Japanese food.

The Man of Zen who practices Karate obviously is the adventurous type; and Sensei, staying true to type, enjoyed participating in Beryl's and George's investigations. It required little time for him to become a one-third partner of the team. He called himself, "the ampersand in Wagner & Tilson."

Sensei Wong may have been better at advertising karate than at performing it, but this merely says that he was a superb huckster for the discipline. In college he had studied civil engineering; but he also was on the fencing team and he regularly practiced gymnastics. He had learned yoga and ancient forms of meditation from his mother. He attained Zen's vaunted transcendental states; which he could access 'on the mat.' It was not surprising that when he began to learn karate he was already half-accomplished. After he won a few minor championships he attracted the attention of several martial arts publications that found his "unprecedented" switchings newsworthy. They imparted to him a "great master" cachet, and perpetuated it to the delight of dojo owners and martial arts shopkeepers. He did win many championships and, through unpaid endorsements and political propaganda, inspired the sale of Japanese weapons, including nunchaku and shuriken which he did not actually use.

Although his Order was strongly given to celibacy, enough wiggle room remained for the priest who found it expedient to marry or dally. Yet, having reached his mid-forties unattached, he regarded it as 'unlikely' that he would ever be romantically welded to a female, and as 'impossible' that he would be bonded to a citizen and custom's agent of the People's Republic of China - whose Gung Fu abilities challenged him and who would strike terror in his heart especially when she wore Manolo Blahnik red spike heels. Such combat, he insisted, was patently unfair, but he prayed that Providence would not level the playing field. He met his femme fatale while working on A Case of Virga.

Later in their association Sensei would take under his spiritual wing a young Thai monk who had a degree in computer science and a flair for acting. Akara Chatree, to whom Sensei's master in Taiwan would give the name Shi Yao Xin, loved Shakespeare; but his father - who came from one of Thailand's many noble families - regarded his son's desire to become an actor as we would regard our son's desire to become a hit man. Akara's brothers were all businessmen and professionals; and as the old patriarch lay dying, he exacted a promise from his tall 'matinee-idol' son that he would never tread upon the flooring of a stage. The old man had asked for nothing else, and since he bequeathed a rather large sum of money to his young son, Akara had to content himself with critiquing the performances of actors who were less filially constrained than he. As far as romance is concerned, he had not thought too much about it until he worked on A Case of Industrial Espionage. That case took him to Bermuda, and what can a young hero do when he is captivated by a pretty girl who can recite Portia's lines with crystalline insight while lying beside him on a white beach near a blue ocean?

But his story will keep...

# MONDAY, OCTOBER 24, 2011

George Wagner had just about convinced himself and others - strangers mostly - that he had reached the Zen goal of finding transcendent fulfillment in the performance of his daily work. This attainment of Karma Yoga's vaunted state of spiritual deliverance is not a trivial matter in Zen circles; and often, when he was in the temple, sitting on his seiza bench, or in the bar, standing with his foot on the brass rail, people would approach him to ask his advice and, of course, the secret of his success.

On such occasions George would reveal that he employed a slightly altered Sherlock Holmesian dictum: he eliminated all irksome duties and could therefore regard whatever remained, regardless of difficulty, as worthy of his effort. He was an accomplished investigator; and when he accepted a case, no matter how daunting its complexity or confounding its rationale, he performed its labors with contentment and could sigh with the Dao poet:

*How wonderful!*
*How mysterious!*
*I chop wood.*
*I carry water.*

Using the justification that, after all, he neither split atoms nor groomed dogs - since such tasks were better left to more qualified men - he believed it to be a matter of simple common sense to pay someone to do annoying tasks while he concentrated on chopping and carrying an investigation. If Bodhidharma himself appeared to him, saying that picking and choosing the tasks that one cared to perform did not exactly meet the requirements of Karma Yoga's discipline, George would have doubted the wisdom of Zen's founder.

There were times when George Wagner was blind even to Zen's fundamental insight: *peace is not the absence of war.*

It was not, therefore, that the autumn day was too sunny and warm and too pregnant with recreational possibilities that caused George to resist accepting the case. And it was not that he had more challenging and enjoyable work to do. He detested bossy clients, especially the variety who denigrated the study and skill that went into an investigation and said such things as, "You made a few phone calls. How difficult was that?"

Marietta Post had begun the conversation by informing him that he had been very highly recommended as a private investigator. She then asked if he was available to work on a suspicious death case that had been ruled an accident. Flattered, he allowed himself to fall into the trap and said that indeed, he was available and suggested that she come into the office to meet with him. She asked his fee and he quoted it, whereupon she then informed him that the matter was so simple that anyone ought to be able to do it. Perhaps he had an apprentice on his staff whose *per diem* rate was not so excessive? Before George could tell her to call another agency, she said, "Very well, we'll be there," and hung up.

He went to Beryl Tilson's desk in the outer office and groused, "Find something for me to do this morning. If Marietta Post shows up you can handle her any way you want. A woman like that can ruin a man's whole day."

Beryl looked up from the bookkeeping program she was running. "You can organize the bills that have been in your in-box for three weeks, take them down to Sensei so that he can initial them, and then you can write the checks."

George protested. "How come I always get stuck with the bookkeeping. Ain't it your turn? I paid the bills last month."

"Last month was not June. This is October. Don't give me heartburn," she threatened.

Mimicking her words, he returned to his desk and pep-talked himself into doing "office work." As he finally lifted the stack of bills and miscellaneous documents from his in-box, the office door opened. He waited. Beryl said, "Good morning. May I help you?" and a woman's voice answered, "I am Miss Marietta Post and this is my niece Miss Chloe Ingram. We have an appointment with George Wagner. Kindly tell him that we are here." George groaned and let the papers fall back into the box.

To Beryl, the women were improbably odd. The older one seemed like one of those brisk, all-business dog trainers who was taking the younger one, an old arthritic beagle, for a walk. The leash was a short one. Beryl quickly positioned a second chair in front of her desk.

"Sit," said the older woman, poking the younger one who plopped into the chair with a jolt that caused her eyeglasses to bounce down her nose. The older woman put her index finger against the eyeglass bridge and shoved the glasses back, dislodging, as she did, one stringy tress of hair that Beryl thought had been fused to the others after weeks of not being washed. The dirt-stiff hair stuck out at an unnatural angle. Beryl found the young woman's appearance disturbing. Ms. Post sat down and waited.

On the other side of the partition, George was "cornered." Ordering himself to be professional, he got up from his desk and walked to the opening. "That was fast," he said. "You must have called from across the street–" He had intended to invite the two women to come into his office, but after getting a closer look at Chloe Ingram, he decided not to risk an unpleasant result by asking her to move. "I'll bring my chair in here and we can discuss the problem." With that, he wheeled one of his office chairs into the front office and sat beside Beryl.

Miss Post returned Beryl's disapproving glare as she explained her problem. "My sister Catherine was a lady of great distinction. You are no doubt aware of her charitable efforts. Catherine met her death on the first day of this month in Lake George, New York, in what was officially called an accident. My niece thinks that her stepfather murdered her mother."

Beryl thought it unlikely that the girl was capable of any cognitive function. "Your niece seems to be heavily sedated," she said.

"Yes. She is disconsolate." She tugged on Chloe's sleeve. "Tell them how disconsolate you are, my dear."

Chloe Ingram looked at her sleeve but said nothing.

"I believe," said Miss Post, "that tranquilizers are holding her together. Without them she will fall apart."

Beryl bristled at the girl's mistreatment. "What is the tranquilizer?" she asked. "Formaldehyde?" The remark was rude, but she did not regret making it.

Marietta Post sniffed the air and looked at George. "I'd prefer to speak to you privately."

Seated in the relative privacy of George's side of the partition, Marietta Post began to lay out the bare bones of the case, pausing as she named each piece to consider where it should fit into the skeletal design.

George was familiar with the story. Because Catherine Post Ingram Pavano had been married to a local man, Bill Pavano, who was a member of a slightly notorious family, the Philadelphia newspapers took more notice of her death than they probably would have taken. She had devoted years of her life to calling the world's attention to the plight of its most wretched poor, the refugees of war who lived in squalid tents and silently starved, succumbing to diseases that elsewhere would have been cured.

It was not, however, her philanthropy that caused the newspapers to devote a few column inches of front page space to her death. It was an embarrassing glitch in the funeral arrangements that cast a peculiar and, therefore, newsworthy light on her demise. She had wished to be interred in her family plot in a small upstate town after a Requiem Mass had been celebrated. But despite her charitable works and her financial support of several Catholic institutions, the parish priests had unanimously declined to celebrate such a Mass since, they noted, after having been married in a Nuptial Mass, the occasion in which Catherine Post became

Mrs. Dwight Ingram, she had agreed to give Ingram a divorce; and after that purely civil agreement, she had married Bill Pavano, the operator of a Lake George yoga center. The priests did not object to Pavano's teaching the exercise of yoga. They did deplore his Hindu affectations; his exotic "holy man" garments; his wearing of floral leis; his teaching of chants and prayers to bizarre gods; and his display of symbolically pornographic artifacts in his cult's "temple."

The local Ordinary could not restrain their imaginations from foreseeing the heretical Pavano, who had been confirmed a Catholic as a boy, invading the sanctity of consecrated space in order to lead his followers in disgusting rituals at her grave. They regretted that a few liberal priests in Italy, of all places, had allowed Catherine to marry Pavano in a church. Rather than risk internecine strife with their revisionist brethren, the priests advised Pavano to ship her remains overseas and to appeal to those who "ministered to apostates" for assistance. For Catherine Post Ingram Pavano there would be neither funeral service in their church nor interment in their cemetery.

Pavano protested, but after a week of pointless argument, during which Catherine's body reposed in a refrigerator, he had her cremated. The once imagined solemn procession of cars, with their headlights on in broad daylight, did not occur. The grand cortege was replaced by a delivery man's placing of a model #3222 Bronze Urn into Pavano's hands, subsequent to the less than solemn signing of a clip-board receipt.

George knew that the print media's interest in Catherine Pavano's postmortem affairs had already withered and died; but now, Catherine's sister and daughter were sitting in a private investigator's office with the vivifying allegation that Pavano had actually murdered his wife. George saw an opportunity. He would have a "way out," an escape clause, if the case had a sensational aspect. "Has Miss Ingram reported her suspicions to the police or discussed it with anyone?" he asked.

"No. We desire privacy." Miss Post punctuated her desire with a sarcastic question. "Would I have hired a private investigator if I intended to make a public declaration of this suspicion of murder?"

"I don't know what you would have done," George said. "I know only that if it is an open police case, we cannot get involved. Mr. Pavano and his relatives are fairly well known in this city. If your suspicions have begun to make their way to the local press, we might find this office besieged with journalists who would then make any 'private' investigation impossible."

"My niece's suspicions are unknown to anyone but me and now you. Can we get on with it?"

George leaned forward on his elbows, wondering how much more of Marietta Post he could take before her abrasive personality scraped-off what was left of his civility. "As I recall from the press accounts, your sister drove off a cliff–"

"Cliff seems overdramatic," Miss Post corrected him. "The road's elevation at that point was only sixty feet. Still, it was enough. Chloe is certain that her step-father had arranged the accident."

"Sixty feet is like a six storey building. As I recall he was in their hilltop home at the time, celebrating his birthday party."

"And you think that because he wasn't in the car with her, he couldn't have arranged the so-called accident?" she challenged.

"No. I don't think anything, yet. By all accounts, they were happily married for fifteen years. Did anything occur that might have given him a motive?"

"He had finally succeeded in getting her to write a new will. Previously her estate was divided between her two children, Chloe and her brother Morgan Ingram; and there was a substantial provision for me to enable me to continue my work on behalf of our Holy Church. The new will gave him half of her estate and the other half was divided between Chloe and Morgan. Any monies I received would be at the discretion of Mr. Pavano. Gaining his inheritance - some forty million dollars - is a rather strong motive, I should think."

So far the only motive that George could determine was Marietta Post's motive for supporting her niece's suspicion. He tried to explain. "It's a common mistake to assume that the person who has the most to gain is the one who is most likely to kill for it. The person who will inherit ten million dollars and who wants that money badly doesn't care that by his action he will enrich someone else who will inherit twenty million... especially when he knows that people make the mistake of assuming that the one who has the most to gain is the one who is most likely to have committed the crime!" George was getting irritated. "Of course, there are people who can hate the recipient of a larger sum so much that they'd forego..."

Beryl coughed and cleared her throat in the outer office. George knew that he was starting to sound idiotic. He answered the cough and cleared his throat. "You need more than suspicion to sustain a charge. Did they have an argument?"

"None that I know of."

"Was she seeing a therapist for any psychological distress? Did a toxicology report find any substances in her blood that may have affected her ability to drive safely?"

Miss Post was offended by the idea that anyone would even ask if her sister was getting psychotherapy. "Certainly not. My sister's mind was both sturdy and pure of any taint. The report indicated only a slight amount of alcohol and no drugs of any kind. She joined in a toast... a single glass of champagne... to her husband's health and prosperity."

"Miss Post, given that your sister created this festive birthday occasion for her husband of fifteen years, and that she was not being treated in any way for psychological distress, and that everyone who knew them agreed that they were happy, he doesn't seem to have a motive. Add that to the fact that they operated together their herbal supplement business which he had founded and that they were considered 'a power couple' in the industry, all Mr. Pavano had to do to defeat her old will, was to get a lawyer... any lawyer. He'd have gotten half her estate with no problem. He didn't need to wait for her to write a new will. Were there any insurance policies on her life?"

"Catherine had assumed that if anything happened to her while her children were young, their father, Dwight Ingram, would become their guardian. She therefore made him the beneficiary of five million dollars worth of insurance on her life."

George cleared his throat again. "In the annals of murder, five million in insurance on an ex-wife would constitute an incentive. But why, since you obviously care about her children, didn't she name you as beneficiary or trustee?" It occurred to George that she was perhaps trying to implicate Ingram and that the charge against Pavano was a ploy of some kind.

"My sister did not charge me with the guardianship of her children because, Mr. Wagner, I was and am a Roman Catholic nun. My true name is Sister Marie Paul. As a nun I was and am hardly in a position to raise children. I am in mufti today for obvious reasons. I am the directress of a shelter for unwed mothers, *The Little Flower's Haven*. We are located on the southeast coast of Maine."

George could not discern the obvious reasons that kept her from wearing a nun's habit, but he said, "I understand." He ran his fingers through his hair and sat back. "Is there anything more substantive to the suspicion? Another woman perhaps?"

Miss Post laughed. "Hardly that!" she said in a voice that was loaded with accusation.

"A little history would be helpful," George said.

"Briefly, then, after Catherine and Dwight Ingram had been married some eight years, Dwight had an affair with his secretary. He had gotten the woman pregnant and wanted a divorce. My sister had at first refused to consider a divorce, but when she learned of the existence of an innocent child, she relented.

"At the time, Chloe was five and Morgan was seven. The divorce was, in a manner of speaking, a seller's market. Catherine received a substantial settlement which she wisely invested in electronics and pharmaceuticals. The money didn't come from Dwight. The secretary's family did not want their grandchild born out of wedlock. They were desperate to salvage what was left of the wretched girl's reputation and liquidated most of their assets to provide it. What little Dwight Ingram earned he squandered on his new family and on other bad investments.

"The divorce was stressful. Catherine developed back problems. Kneeling in prayer, for example, became difficult. On the advice of her physician, she took yoga lessons in a Hindu ashram - one of those meeting places of so-called 'religions.' Bill Pavano, although only twenty, was the resident high priest or 'guru' as they are called. The exercises helped.

"Pavano's devotees claimed to be spiritually cleansed by him. I suppose eating raw bean sprouts and drinking wheat grass juice were effective penances.

"What is more to the point is that he also huckstered herbal nostrums which people raved about. Catherine could always see the wise and ignore the foolish. She saw the salubrious effects of these inexpensive medicines, and her mission became clear. What better way to help the poor?

"She admired Pavano, and since he was handsome and strong, he became the perfect escort for her in her ministry. Within a year of starting yoga with him, she married him.

"He told her that she brought stability to his life. She thought he meant emotional stability. Actually, it was financial. He owed everybody money. She paid all his debts and expanded his product lines. He cultivated a taste for Kobe beef and caviar. Yes, he burned all those vegetarian menus and rose like a wolf from the ashes - a peculiarly tame wolf." She stopped her narrative and searched her mind for a word. "What do you call a female wolf?"

"That would be 'a bitch,'" George offered.

"Indeed," Marietta Post sniffed the air again. "With him at her side, she became a formidable champion of war refugees. They practically lived on a boat as they sailed from one refugee camp to the next. She took photographs and gave lectures to any group who would listen. Magazine articles were written about her. She founded several charities."

George blinked. The "boat" she was referring to was a three-tiered twenty-five million dollar yacht currently docked in Philadelphia. "She sounds like a great lady."

"Yes," Miss Post continued, "a great Catholic lady. As such she did not have a sexual relationship with Mr. Pavano. Her vows were carved into the rock of a Nuptial Mass. She could not break them. Mr. Wagner, my sister lived the life of a saint. I often told her that she was married to the Gospels. Pavano was not so inspired. He liked men, and she could hardly change that. She did insist that he be discreet. She would not tolerate scandal or any of that flamboyant nonsense."

George was puzzled. "How old was Pavano when she married him?" he asked.

"I already told you! He was twenty. She was thirty-two. She gave him his 35th birthday party in their 'on land' home which my sister had gotten in the divorce. It's called Ingram House. It's located on top of a hill near Lake George... hence, the 'cliff,' as you call it."

"Does your niece have a theory about how he committed this murder?"

"She believes that Pavano did it with the help of the housekeeper, Mrs. Danvers. Her real name is Ruth Blackhawk. He called her Danvers because he thought it sounded more elegant. Perhaps he was in a *Rebecca* phase of development. Under the terms of the previous will, Danvers would have received one hundred thousand dollars a year for life. Under the new will, her pension is left to the discretion of Mr. Pavano."

"And you think she helped him to murder his wife just to stay on his good side?" George wanted to laugh. "That makes no sense. If she assisted him and he bungled the job, she'd be charged as his accomplice. If he succeeded without her, she could turn him in. The old will would have been reinstated. She'd be better off."

"If? And if he had friends that would guarantee her silence? If he had not wanted to give her a nickel, she would not have gotten a cent."

"Aren't you in the same financial predicament as the housekeeper?"

"Are you accusing me of complicity in my sister's murder?"

George had had enough. "I'm sorry. I don't think I can help you. You've said someone recommended me and I'm sorry to disappoint that person... whoever it was." He was preparing to stand up when Chloe Ingram's eyes widened and her lips moved, forming the word, "Don't!"

George rubbed his face. "Look," he said in a conciliatory manner, "you shouldn't start naming accomplices until you've settled on the principal actor." He did not know Bill Pavano, yet he found himself sympathizing with him. There was too much that was disquieting about the case. He looked at Chloe and tried to reconcile her status as an heiress with her appearance as a derelict. "You'll have to tell me more... more that makes sense. Pavano stood to gain millions in the future, but he was not without present resources. He was in a position to pay for any kind of help he needed to commit the crime. Only a fool would have involved a servant who had a financial interest in the outcome."

"Nevertheless, that is what my niece suspects."

"Then she should go to the police."

"She wanted to, but I persuaded her not to antagonize him. So much now depends on his charitable mood. Six months or so ago, Mr. Pavano suddenly displayed an interest in my institution, that is to say, The Little Flower's Haven. We had always taught basic baby care," she explained, "but he thought we should expand and teach these girls marketable skills - such as typing, computer operation, English composition, and so on. The goal was to make them self-sufficient. He thought that a clerical job would raise their self-esteem," she snickered, "as if knowing how to type inoculates a young woman against immorality. He thought these women would be able to earn enough money to keep their babies. Since the expansion was his idea, he wanted to be able to manage and care for it."

"Ah, I see. His involvement in the project influenced your sister to give him greater discretionary power. He can give you whatever he thinks is needed to carry out the program." Bill Pavano was becoming more admirable with each new bit of information. "But if Miss Ingram makes such a charge against him and it fails, and you are seen as her ally, he might refuse to place into your hostile hands any money at all."

"Precisely. Which is why we've come to you."

"I understand why you haven't gone to the police, but I don't see the reason for suspecting him in the first place. He sounds like a decent enough fellow."

"He has cleverly orchestrated the 'sound' of decency. In fact, he is a narcissistic beast. Do you think he cares about unborn babies? A half-dozen years ago, Chloe, here, got involved with a local boy who worked in a gas station, a rough boy who took advantage of her. She was only sixteen and he got her pregnant. Ruth Danvers discovered this when she saw Chloe having morning sickness. She told Bill Pavano and he literally forced Chloe to have an abortion. He said that if she refused, he would have the boy charged with statutory rape. The boy had some sentimental regard for his offspring and when he learned that she had had an abortion, he became furious. Ultimately, he was persuaded to join the Army."

"Didn't your sister object? Wouldn't that have violated her religious beliefs?"

"Of course!" Miss Post snapped. "If she had known about it, I'm sure it would have! Pavano was a snob. He came from an old Florentine family, or so he claimed. The gas station boy was of Sicilian stock. Pavano would not countenance the presence of a Sicilian on the family tree."

"But that was years ago. The pregnancy was terminated. How does that give Pavano a motive to murder his wife then or now?"

Marietta Post's anger began to rise. "Chloe did not attend the party! She was conducting research somewhere in the Adirondacks. She is getting her master's degree in geology. But during the party Catherine received a call that purported to be from Chloe. Catherine left the party because she believed that Chloe was injured or ill at the base of the hill. Catherine borrowed Danvers's car - her own was blocked by guest parking. She said that Chloe had wanted her to come quickly since she was afraid that some meddling bystander would call 9-1-1. My sister didn't want the party spoiled so she left. On her way down, in her haste, she drove over the edge and plunged to her death. The problem, Mr. Wagner, is that Chloe insists that she made no such call."

George shook his head. "How do you know what they said to each other - Catherine and this fake Chloe?"

Marietta Post's nostrils flared. "We know what was said because Catherine told Danvers what the call was about when she borrowed her car."

"On one hand you suspect Danvers of helping to murder Catherine and on the other you accept whatever she tells you. What specifically did Catherine tell Danvers?"

"I just told you!"

George's intercom button on his desk phone pulsed red. He excused himself and answered. Beryl ran the printer and whispered, "How is it that Catherine was fooled by an impostor's voice?"

George pretended it was a routine office call. "Just tell him I'll call him later." He hung up the phone and turned to Miss Post. "How is it that Catherine was tricked by an imposter's voice? Didn't she know her own daughter's voice when she heard it?"

Miss Post responded with vehement sarcasm. "Well, now... an injured child's voice could never be *distorted by pain*... or, a weakened voice on a telephone could never be drowned out by the *ambient noise of a room filled with boisterous friends playing the piano and singing show tunes!*"

George sighed. "Who discovered the accident?"

"Chloe's brother Morgan." Miss Post had nearly run out of patience. "When he realized that he hadn't seen his mother in a while, he asked Danvers; and then he went to look for Catherine. He saw the tire tracks that went off the road. He looked over the edge and saw the car below. Its lights were still on. By the grace of God there was no fire. But we are not interested in who discovered the crime, *we are interested in who perpetrated it!*"

George ignored the remark. "Were Morgan, Pavano, and Danvers all present at the party, before and after Catherine went out?"

"Yes! That was established!" Marietta Post seemed ready to whack George's hands with a ruler. She stiffened. After a long pause, she said, "We want you to prove that my sister was murdered by Bill Pavano!"

On the other side of the partition, Beryl coughed loudly.

George tried to be diplomatic. "Was anything suspicious noted at autopsy?"

"No!" She brought her purse down on the edge of his desk. "See here! Do you want the case or not?"

"Madam... Sister..." Just as George decided that there was no possible way he would get involved in such a totally unfounded proposition, he saw Chloe Ingram's eyes widen and blink and her lips form the word, "Please."

"Ah," he said, "Lake George is not around the corner. You do realize that it will be very expensive to bring out-of-state investigators in."

Miss Marietta Post had passed the point of tolerance. She shouted, "I speak to you of the loss of millions and you want to warn me about travel time and motel room rates! Are you some kind of dunce?"

Beryl had also reached a limit. She had an irrepressible urge to laugh. She coughed again and gulped in a useless attempt to stifle a giggle. She got up from her desk and went outside to laugh openly, standing on the sidewalk. George looked up when he heard the office door open and close.

Miss Post was indignant. "Can you not get it through your head that my niece is seeking justice? It is more than a matter of simple academic interest to learn whether one's mother died accidentally or whether she was deliberately murdered. It is not useless information to be filed away with recipes for blueberry pie as those who are allergic to blueberries might do!"

George looked at Chloe Ingram. "I understand. We'll be happy to investigate the matter immediately. We can be at Lake George tomorrow. We'll need a signed agency agreement." He opened a drawer and withdrew several copies of a standard contract. "I see no need to call my partner in here. I'll fill out the document, myself. We'll also require a twenty thousand dollar retainer. Is that satisfactory?"

Marietta Post took out a checkbook. George cautioned, "I can't accept your check. The retainer must come from the client, your niece."

"This," she said defiantly, "*is* my niece's check book!" She filled out the check, put the pen into Chloe's hand and tried to help her to write. George watched as Chloe shook off the older woman's hand and carefully signed the check.

"Then we are agreed," George said. "If indeed Catherine Pavano was murdered, we shall do all that is humanly possible to discover who murdered her, as well as how and why the murder was committed. We'll furnish detailed time and expense accounts and return to you any sums not spent." He signed the documents and placed them in front of Chloe, indicating where they should be signed. Again, with no help, she signed her name.

Marietta Post stood up. "I must return to my duties tonight. I will take my niece home to Lake George immediately. Her address is on the check. From this point on, I will have nothing to do with this matter." She tugged again at Chloe's sleeve, and the girl picked up her copy of the contract, stood up, and followed her aunt out of the office.

As the door closed behind them, George walked into the front office and waited for Beryl to return.

She entered and called, "Walk-ees," imitating an English lady who used to teach dog training on TV. "Walk-ees in mufti!"

George tossed the contract and check on her desk. "Ber," he said, "that woman called me a dunce." He finally was able to laugh. "Take a look! Our moribund client signed these."

Beryl looked at the clearly written signatures. "If Chloe Ingram signed these, we've got a good actress on our hands."

"We have to drive up to Lake George tonight. Tomorrow, we will let the show begin."

# TUESDAY, OCTOBER 25, 2011

The map indicated that the distance between Philadelphia and Lake George was two hundred fifty miles which George thought were best traveled at night if they wanted to avoid metropolitan rush hours. They had gotten all they could from internet resources. George had asked an old friend at the police department to check out Bill Pavano, and the report had come back, "His sheet is clean."

At 3 a.m. they checked into a double room at the Lago Motel in Lake George. Since there was no point in getting up early, they slept until nine o'clock. After breakfast they checked in with the local police.

By intercom, the desk sergeant informed Captain Ross D'Angelo that he had visitors; and the captain called out from his office, "Don't stand on ceremony! The season's over. Ain't nobody here but us chickens."

George and Beryl walked back to his office. As they appeared in his doorway, he stood up and extended his hand. He was tall, slim and erect, with Roman features and short curled hair that imparted such dignity that a sculptor would have wanted to crown his head with laurel. He extended his hand and George showed his damaged right hand as he extended his left in a fist which the captain likewise met in a fraternal "bump" salute.

Beryl put their business card on his desk. "We're here about the Pavano death," George said.

"Ah," said D'Angelo, reading the card, "Have a seat, George. You a former 'man with a badge'?"

"Homicide, Philadelphia Police," George answered. "Injured in the line of etcetera, etcetera."

"Tough break, my brother." He nodded and put his hands behind his head. "I was wondering how long it would take before that accident was questioned."

"Why were you wondering?" George asked.

"Money. Big money. Older woman, younger man. The usual formulas for suspicion. Who's your client?"

Beryl answered "Confidentially, Chloe Ingram. How did Catherine and Pavano get along?"

"We never had any problem with them. But then, they were away from here most of the time. But Chloe had some problems with him over a boyfriend."

"The boy at the gas station?" Beryl asked.

"Yeah, that's the one. Who told you about Dan Brancati?"

"Chloe's aunt."

"I haven't seen that woman up close in twenty years. I hear she's become quite the shrike."

George grinned. "She impaled me until I took the case. Yes, she could be morphing into one of those. Actually, she's a nun, the directress of a home for unwed mothers."

"A directress? I knew she had become a nun, but I didn't know her title." D'Angelo nodded, "She always was religious. I thought she'd be around for the funeral, but I guess you know there wasn't one. Chloe's brother is here in town. Morgan. He's up at the house with her and Bill Pavano. He's been here since before the party."

"We didn't get much information about Morgan," Beryl said. "What's he like?"

"He's some kind of genius. A Ph.D. in Physics. Dr. Morgan Ingram. A bit too full of himself. He prefers to be called 'Doctor Ingram.' Other than that, he's ok. But what do you really know about anybody?" He leaned on his desk. "What can I do you for?"

"Was there anyone or anything suspicious about the accident?" Beryl asked.

D'Angelo scratched his chin. "We couldn't find any reason to suspect foul play. Her car had not been tampered with. And trust me, we checked that car. It didn't burn in the collision. Alcohol was not a factor. She had maybe one glass of wine. There were no other drugs in her system."

"Which in a way supports the idea that the marriage was not on the rocks," Beryl noted.

"Exactly. The tox tests just came back. No mood altering medications were present. She wasn't depressed and she was sleeping well. Say, I've got pictures in here," he turned on his computer. "Morgan took them at the party. They've been officially tagged as possible evidence - of what, nobody's sure - so I'm not at liberty to send you copies. But Morgan has them and as long as he's on your side, I'm sure he'll give you a set."

The photographs revealed Catherine to be a remarkably beautiful woman. In one striking photo, a man, whose back was to the camera, was bent forward as he kissed her hand so that her gently smiling face could clearly be seen. She wore no makeup or so little of it that it did not show. Except for a few long wispy curls on either side of her face, her hair, a soft ash blonde, was pulled back into a braid that spiraled at the back of her head. Jeweled ribbons that hung from the braid created a sort of medieval hairstyle. She wore a long black velvet dress that, except for its deep square neckline, covered her arms and back. She wore no jewelry except for a wedding ring and a gold chain that supported a pendant cross. In photographs of her taken away from the group, she was posed with a man in eight shots: two were with Bill and six were with an overweight man.

"The young guy is her husband?" George asked.

"Yep. That's Bill Pavano. The fat guy is an executive of their Shivadas herbal medicine company. He's also a director of her charitable foundations. His name is Cardinale."

"Cardinale looks like he's in love with her. And frankly, she is looking up at him with a flirtatious expression."

"Greed, probably," D'Angelo whispered. "Catherine liked money and that guy is supposed to be rich."

"Who's at the house now?" George asked.

"Bill Pavano; Morgan Ingram, make that Dr. Morgan Ingram; Chloe Ingram; the housekeeper, Ruth Danvers; and that's about all I can think of. I'm not absolutely certain that they're all there. I called the house a couple of days ago when I got the tox report and that seemed to be the roll call. Do you want to go look at the accident scene?"

"Sure," George said, standing up. "That's what we're here for." He led the way out of the captain's office.

"Just a second!" D'Angelo called. "I don't want to offend you, but I notice that you have a little limp."

"Yes," said George. "I took one in the shoulder and another in the knee. Usually it doesn't show, but the motel bed was not exactly accommodating."

"I was going to suggest that we park at the base of the hill and walk up since parking at the scene of the accident is hazardous. Not many cars come down that road, but when they do, it can be hairy. I don't think you'll want to walk up, so how about if we take my official motorcycle and sidecar, and Miss Tilson here, who I see is wearing long pants, can hop on the back of the Harley. I can park the cycle at the side of the road."

George got into the sidecar, and though he felt foolish sitting in it, the road soon made him glad that he had agreed. He estimated that the road's inclination was at least eight degrees.

They pulled off just before they came to the accident's site markers. "It's amazing," said the captain, "we've had no rain since the accident. The road is just about as it was." He pointed to ruts in the dirt that showed precisely where the car had plunged over the cliff.

"What kind of car was she driving?" Beryl asked.

"It was the housekeeper's car. A 1986 Chrysler Town and Country station wagon. She kept it in mint condition, but it had a long chassis and tended to be loose."

George explained, "By 'loose' the captain means--"

"I follow NASCAR," Beryl said indignantly. "I know what he means. The car fishtails."

"Sorr-ry!" George said. He turned to D'Angelo. "Women nowadays are not the way they used to be. They used to be sweet and dumb. Now they're mean and smart."

"You won't get any argument from me," D'Angelo said.

They walked up to the place where the tire marks indicated that Catherine had begun to swerve towards the outside of the road.

"Are trucks allowed to use this road?" George asked.

"No. Absolutely not," D'Angelo answered. "The Ingrams or Pavanos use this road exclusively. There are only two other houses up on the hill and they own both of 'em. On the other side of the hill, there's a new road that goes back down to the highway in a gentle slope. It's like what they call 'fault mountains' or 'thrust up mountains,' which means the earth's crust pushed one side straight up, but the back side slopes down gently. The mountains of Tibet are supposed to be like that. Straight up on the Everest side and then a long slope down for miles on the China side. I don't know what I'm talking about, but you understand. The Ingram House is the oldest house. Traffic to the other houses would have to pass in front of it if this switchback road were used. Fortunately, for the Ingram's privacy, nobody else bothers much with this road. Most visitors or tradespeople use the back road. It's longer, but safer."

"Were they expecting any more guests or deliveries at the party?" Beryl asked.

"That was my point. I asked and they said they weren't. So something or somebody who was not expected must have come up, and she swerved to avoid hitting him."

Beryl walked along the inside of the road. She held up her hand to stop the others. "At this point, as Catherine came down she'd be on this side of the road. The inside, her right. Then suddenly she veers off to her left as if something's coming at her in her lane. But there are no tire marks on this side of the road that would indicate that an oncoming vehicle tried to avoid *her* by turning to *its* right. The hill meets the road at a perpendicular. Neither vehicle could have turned into it to avoid an oncoming car. Why didn't the oncoming car react to her headlights as she reacted to its headlights? Since no car was reported to have reached the top, and there doesn't seem to be a place for a car to turn around in, I'd say that there was no other car at all."

"The investigators figured that, too. We have lots of deer up here," D'Angelo replied. "They assumed that she swerved to avoid hitting one."

"Yes," Beryl countered, "but when is the last time a deer telephoned Catherine Ingram Pavano and pretended to be her daughter?"

"Mean and smart," said George. "I told you, mean and smart."

"I'll tell you what I think," Beryl said. "I think there was a phantom car. Maybe somebody rigged two headlights with a battery. As she passed some kind of electronic control beam, a little farther up the road, Catherine activated the headlights, and then she was suddenly blinded by them and swerved to get out of the way of what she thought was an oncoming car. Do you remember Princess Diana's accident? One investigator theorized that a paparazzi on a motorcycle pulled in front of her car. There was probably a passenger on the cycle who was able to turn and look back to get the shot, and in the dark tunnel they were in, his camera flash blinded her driver and made him lose control. The same situation could have occurred with Catherine. It was night. She couldn't have seen more than the headlights. She swerved to avoid what she thought was a head-on collision."

"That," said the captain emphatically, "makes one hell of a lot more sense than anything else I've heard about this case. And then whoever set it up, could just remove two goddamned headlights and a battery. Hell, he could have put them in a backpack and walked back to the party or gone down the hill. Let's go up and see if we can find any indication of that remote control device."

George and D'Angelo walked along the inside gully searching for evidence. Beryl walked to the outside of the road. "It would have to be around here or somewhere higher," she said, "on the outside of the road. If it were on the inside, she might have run over it. No, the only safe place would be on the outside. The road is very narrow."

George could tell that the Captain wanted to be the one who discovered evidence of the remote control device. "I'll stay on the inside, just in case. Why don't you lend another pair of eyes to the outside of the road?"

"Good idea," D'Angelo said, crossing to the outside to join Beryl at the road's edge. Beryl got behind him.

For fifty feet or so they scoured the roadside; and then D'Angelo shouted, "Look! Look at this!" He pointed to several stones that had been placed in a U configuration. Marks in the dirt indicated that something had been placed inside the U and that the stones were probably positioned to keep it in place. "Lemme get my phone!" he exclaimed, pulling his cellphone from his pocket. "This is where the remote control beam was put. Goddamn! Let's get this from every angle before it rains."

Beryl reached into her tote bag and withdrew a camcorder. "Here, you can make it official. The date and time are accurate."

"Thank God I can say I found the stone supports," said D'Angelo. "Shoot me first and make sure the audio is on." Beryl filmed him as he gave name, place, and the theory of the phantom car. He explained the use of "other than regulation" equipment and personnel, and he mentioned the assistance of licensed private investigators Beryl Tilson and George Wagner, "a *decorated* homicide investigator formerly with the Philadelphia Police." He continued to comment as he took the camera and documented the entire scene, including his discovery of the possible location of the electronic beam mechanism, the ruts, and his opinion of the location of the battery and headlights. He returned the camera to Beryl and turned to George. "I'm gonna stand tall in Albany! You'll give me a copy of that?"

"As soon as we get back to your office," she assured him.

"Wha'dya feed her?" he asked George.

"Raw meat. It keeps her lean and mean."

Using this new theory about the 'means' of the crime, they decided to re-think the case before going to the Ingram House. Ross D'Angelo called and ordered a couple of pizzas and a six- pack of Coke. When they returned to the police station, he asked the desk sergeant to pick up the order in another ten minutes.

George issued a warning. "We need to beef-up this headlights theory. So far, we only *suspect* how it was done. We don't have the remote control device or the headlights. The perp may have decided to keep them. It isn't as if the murder weapon was a knife or gun. But if he hears about this theory, he'll get rid of them. Also, since it doesn't take a genius to rig the whole setup, anybody with a motive could have done it with or without an accomplice. Who knows? The kid in the gas station could have done it, and so could your desk sergeant."

D'Angelo leaned back. "So who's on our Christmas List? All right," he said. "First, the husband. With or without motive, he'd be the prime suspect." He smiled. "I'm getting a kick out of this. I'm really glad you guys are here. My investigative instincts got dull," he lamented. "Everything's so high tech now. It's chemists and biologists who solve all the crimes. Investigators depend on them instead of considering the old 'motive, means, and opportunity.' What's the DNA? Pull his LUDS. Run the prints through IAFIS. Who needs a detective?

"Opportunity isn't limited to the people who were present at the party, but we can start with them and look at their motives, one by one."

"Pavano's supposed to have cheated on Catherine... and not with other women. That's according to the formidable Miss Post," George began the list.

"That's common knowledge," said D'Angelo. "He and the guy who owns Shira Ski Lodge over in Vermont were an item. The Lodge is profitable, but not in any major way. Pavano's boyfriend might have wanted to help the inheritance along, but Catherine had told Bill that his inheritance would be placed in trust for him. The Trustee was that Cardinale, the heavy-set guy in the photographs. So Bill had no motive. He got paid as an executive of that Shivadas herbal company. Big bonuses at the end of the year. And he also collected salary as an administrator of the charities. His employment contracts had tough morality clauses. Catherine was the big money-generator for the charities. In public they were a happily married couple. In private they were good friends. She was a great 'beard' for him. No, Bill didn't want to see her dead.

"Ruth Danvers, the housekeeper, was in the same boat as Marietta Post. They were at the mercy of Bill Pavano. Both of those women are rock hard. I don't see anybody with half a brain conspiring with Pavano. And not his ski buddy, Wes Richter, either. Wes loved three things: his family, Bill, and that ski lodge. As long as Bill got doled out his money regularly, there was a constant stream of cash to keep his family in respectable digs and to keep his ski lodge afloat. If Bill got the money all at once, Bill would suddenly move into a higher social sphere. You know... the euphoria of becoming an overnight millionaire."

"What's this about Wes's family?" Beryl asked.

"Sad case. His wife hit a tree doing some downhill racing. Got busted up bad... paralyzed and brain damaged. From what I've heard Bill pays for her care in some kind of nursing home. Wes has two kids with her. They live with her parents. No. Wes was contented with the status quo. Why risk invoking that morals' clause? He would not have wanted to have Catherine killed.

"Chloe and Morgan? Nah. While Bill's money was held in trust, they got theirs outright. They don't like Pavano; but they're both too smart to risk their fortune and freedom just for the pleasure of seeing him richer or poorer than he already was. Besides, because Catherine was away so much, she had set up big accounts for them... trusts... annuities. Their incomes were just fine with or without her Last Will and Testament."

Beryl asked, "What about the kid from the gas station. Has he continued his relationship with Chloe?"

"Danny Brancati is no kid, Miss Tilson. How much do you know about that trouble with Chloe?"

"Marietta Post filled us in - and with absolutely no finesse. She blurted it out right in front of the girl who's supposed to be suffering emotionally."

"I'm not surprised. Those sisters had a cruel streak. You know how psychopaths can fool a polygraph because they actually believe their own lies, well, that's how they were.

"Danny was heartbroken when he found out Chloe had gotten rid of his kid. Damned shame. He got a little violent and was given the choice between jail or the Army. He was gone for three years. He got married and has two kids, but he's miserable. He's been back at the gas station for the last two years."

"Can you find out if he's seeing Chloe?"

D'Angelo demurred. "I wouldn't confront him. I know he's seeing her. How often or how intimately, I don't know. He's got enough trouble with his marital situation. Does it make a difference?"

George extended the reach of suspicion. "Maybe to his wife. If he was carrying on with Chloe and Chloe suddenly got very rich, they would pay her plenty to get her to agree to a divorce. Sort of like, 'deja vu' all over again... the way her mother took advantage of Dwight Ingram's girlfriend in what Marietta Post called, 'a seller's market.'"

"Danny Brancati's wife has his two kids in Germany. That's where he met and married her. Back here she got the blues and the only medicine that helped her was a ticket to Berlin. She'd have motive but no means or opportunity."

"There's Dwight Ingram, the kids' father. He'd collect about five million in life insurance on Catherine," George said.

"No." D'Angelo was emphatic. "There's no way he killed Catherine. He's a good lookin' guy that women go nuts for... rich women; but he keeps to himself. After his second divorce, he went on a meditation retreat for a couple of months. He came back a different man. He doesn't have two dimes to rub together. I tell him he's like Larry in *The Razor's Edge*. He's martyred to poverty. Of course, that attitude might change now that he's finally able to support a love affair."

"What does he do for a living?" George asked.

"Dwight Ingram? Wait till you see Ingram House. He designed it! He was something else! Twenty-five years ago he had a brilliant future as an architect. I'm not jokin'. After that house, everything was a disaster. His first divorce. His second divorce. His second wife had the baby, a 'special needs' kid who died of pneumonia when he was six years old. Dwight's in-laws tried to get back the money they put up to satisfy Catherine's settlement demands. They claimed they had loaned him the money. He was drowning in the kid's medical bills. He got so disgusted with the human race that he just turned to God. He and his two kids by Catherine had a loving relationship and just knowing that they were ok was enough for him. He stopped trying to become something.

"The computer age finished him off. He was so overwhelmed with personal problems that he never had the free mind to go back to school and learn computer applications... like drafting. Ingram House and the second marriage bankrupted him. Catherine destroyed his reputation. He lost his professional business. Nobody would hire him because he was just 'bad news' and also because he didn't know how to run those architectural computer programs. He's dirt poor now. Lives at the YMCA. But he never took to drink or drugs, and he never got mean. He said to me once, 'Ross, I have accepted my fate.' He does construction work, when he can get it. And I think Chloe and Morgan give him money whenever he needs it."

"What about the nun?"

"I've thought about her. But she had a motive to keep Catherine alive. Sure, maybe if she could pin it on Pavano, she'd kill Catherine. I have a theory about people whose livelihood depends on sponging off other people, including the taxpayer. Dependency begets Entitlement; and a sense of entitlement will justify the most heinous crime, including treason. Murdering your sister is no big deal if you have that dependent personality and think you're *entitled* to what she's got."

"No argument here," George said. "It's true. When people think they're entitled to a bigger share of the pie, no matter how irrational the thought is, they'll kill to get it. All right. We'll keep the nun on our list."

"Let's hear the story about Danny the Sicilian," Beryl said. "Marietta Post told us that Pavano considered himself Florentine nobility and did not appreciate the boy's Sicilian heritage."

"It's amazing," D'Angelo said. "Pavano looks down on any Italian who's not descended from Florentine stock. But the fact is, most of the people in their herbal medicine business are Sicilian. Go figure.

"When Danny found out that Pavano had forced her to have the abortion, he confronted Pavano; but Pavano denied having any part in it. Danny's a good guy. Honest. Dependable. He works for my brother at the gas station. He became a really good mechanic in the Army."

George asked, "Are we sure Chloe doesn't have any other boyfriends to add to the list? And what about Morgan Ingram? And his girlfriends?"

Beryl affected a serious expression. "And the family dog?"

"Ma'am," the captain winked, "if a deer couldn't call Catherine and pretend to be Chloe, the dog sure as hell couldn't have done it."

George grinned. "Ross, have you seen Chloe lately? If she's as comatose as she appears to be, you could believe that a soft- shelled crab called Catherine and pretended to be her. The girl walks around likes she's been embalmed already. Our lean, mean machine here had a few words with Marietta Post. The good Sister said that the girl was on tranquilizers, and she asks her if the tranquilizer was formaldehyde."

The two men were laughing as the desk sergeant returned with the pizza.

At three o'clock in the afternoon, Beryl and George drove up to Ingram House. They reached the crest of the hill and turned to face the house. "Wow!" Beryl gasped. "Look at this place! Amazing!"

George echoed the admiration. "Ross wasn't kidding. This is beautiful."

The summit of the hill, an uneven area of boulder-strewn bedrock and pines, dictated that the structure be narrow, long, and sloping, constraints which the architect followed by creating a curved clear glass and steel ribbed structure that emerged from the ground and widened as it laterally swept upwards like a stretched out chambered nautilus. The shell's aperture lay upon the ground while a concrete slab jutted out from the bedrock to form its terrace and then to become a stark and impressive cantilevered deck which overhung a precipice. Except for the draping branches of a few rosemary bushes, the deck had no decoration or protective railing and seemed to an onlooker to be almost airborne. The afternoon sun dazzled gold on the tall glass panes. The only other colors were supplied by dark rosemary shrubs and pines and scattered clusters of chrysanthemums.

George could see no entrance. "I guess we have to enter it from the other side." Beryl followed the driveway back to the more conventionally designed façade of the glass building. The panes were tall and flat and their wide sections ribbed with steel that seemed to grow, pine tree straight, from out of the bedrock. The glass was not opaque on that side, yet she could not see through it. Instead, it mirrored the distant landscape perfectly. "I guess you get one view of the landscape from inside and two views of it from the outside," she said, turning around.

"I'd like to see this place in the morning," George said as they walked from the parking area to the entrance.

The front door was made of the same reflecting glass. George tried to see inside, but could see nothing but his own image. "The damned thing might as well be made of solid wood," he said, disappointed. He found no doorbell, but yet he could hear one sound inside. "These folks up here like electronic sensors," he groused.

The door easily swung open and Ruth Danvers, much younger by at least twenty years than they had expected her to be, confronted them. She had the exotic look of the tropics, of someone who would look more natural with hibiscus flowers and a sarong than eagle feathers and doeskin.

George handed her his card which she accepted but did not read.

"I'm George Wagner," he said, "and this is my partner, Beryl Tilson. We have an appointment with Miss Chloe Ingram. May we come in?"

"No. Wait here until I check!" the housekeeper snapped, shutting the door. George and Beryl looked at each other and shrugged. It was not a promising reception.

"She's a little too sexy to be a housekeeper," Beryl whispered. "What's going on here?"

After a few interminable minutes, the door opened again. Ruth Danvers returned George's card to him. In a tone that accused George of lying, she sneered, "Miss Ingram doesn't know who you are or what you want. She is not receiving visitors. Please leave quietly."

The aura of peace that had surrounded the house vanished as though it had been a conjurer's illusion. Beryl responded angrily to the woman's hostility. "We are not 'visitors.' We're here by contract and by appointment." Her voice grew more strident. "Go and tell Miss Ingram that we are here!"

A man's voice called, "Danvers! What is this commotion?"

"These people say that they have a contract with Chloe."

"A contract? A contract for what?" Bill Pavano, handsome, blonde, and as statuesque as Michelangelo's *David,* stood in the doorway. He looked at George and repeated, "A contract for what?"

George took a deep breath. "Are you Mr. Pavano?"

Pavano huffed. "You don't come to *my* house and ask *me* questions. I ask the questions. A contract for what?"

George tried to hand Pavano the card that the housekeeper had just returned to him. Pavano glimpsed George's damaged right hand and recoiled in disgust. He would not accept the card and George stood there in the awkward posture of a man who had extended his hand to someone in a respectful greeting and was rebuffed by that person's refusal to shake it. "It's offensive," Pavano said disdainfully. "Wear a glove!"

George could sense Beryl's anger and tried to lessen the tension. "When I was a police officer, I was shot in the shoulder." He held out his left hand, too. "They're no longer a pair," he said, attempting to mitigate the insult's harshness.

"Thank you so much for sharing that," Pavano replied with mock gratitude.

Beryl confronted him. "This is Chloe Ingram's residence! She's over twenty-one and you are *not* her court appointed guardian! Either you get her or I'll assume you're holding her against her will!"

"Get off my property!" Pavano ordered.

George braced himself. He recognized the karate-honed protective instinct that edged Beryl's voice. "Look," he said quietly. "We've come a long way to keep this appointment. Would you please just tell Miss Ingram that we're here?"

Pavano sneered. "Will you two freaks get off my property! Now!" His right arm and shoulder were behind the door. He stepped back so that he could hold the door on its edge and push it shut.

Beryl suddenly kicked the door so hard that it slammed against Pavano's shoulder, wrenching it. The door bounced off him; and before he could shout in pain, she kicked it again and this time it swung back and hit Ruth Danvers squarely in the face. "Go get Chloe Ingram," she hissed, "before I kick your arrogant ass!"

"Call the police!" Pavano shouted at Ruth Danvers who was making little circular movements as she cupped a hand over her bleeding nose. "Call 9-1-1!" he barked.

Beryl stepped into the foyer. "Please do! By all means get the police here for Mr. Pavano. He's the prime subject in our murder investigation! Help us out! Call the police!"

George put his hand on her shoulder. "Calm yourself. Give Mr. Pavano an opportunity to respond." Then he whispered, "What has gotten into you?"

"Danvers!" Pavano shouted. "Forget the police. Show these people into the drawing room and *don't bleed on the rugs*!" His macho demeanor was gone. "You hurt my shoulder!" he whined at Beryl. "I may have a broken bone!"

"Eat more spinach," Beryl advised as she brushed past him.

Another man entered the foyer. "I'm Morgan Ingram, Chloe's brother. May I help you?"

"Dr. Ingram?" Beryl said, deliberately imbuing her tone with awe and respect.

"Why, yes. Have we met?"

"No, I'm afraid we don't travel in M.I.T. circles."

"CalTech, actually."

"Or those."

Dr. Ingram smiled broadly. "You'll have to excuse my stepfather. He's been, shall we say, in a terrible state of bereavement."

"Yes," George said. "We've noticed."

Morgan Ingram led them through the domed drawing room and out onto the cantilevered terrace. "We'll have more privacy out here. And it is a nice day." He gestured towards an arrangement of outdoor furniture. "Please, make yourselves comfortable. I'll see if my sister's awake, but I doubt that she will be."

The deck's construction imparted a feeling of being suspended in space. Beryl walked to the edge. There was nothing but air beneath. "I feel as if I'm on a magic carpet," she said. "Look at this view of the Lake!"

George stood beside her and looked around at the house and view. "Ross D'Angelo said that Ingram could never have killed anyone. I believe it."

Morgan returned, carrying a tray that had three cans of Coke on it. "I could have asked Danvers to make a pitcher of iced tea, but I thought you'd prefer canned Cokes. I know I would."

Beryl laughed. "I trust you eat out often."

"In the month I've been back I don't think I've had any food that I didn't prepare myself." He sat down and invited them to join him. "My sister has been given her medicine. She's too groggy to speak coherently. I can speak for her."

"No," George said, "you can't. It's an 'agent-client' relationship. You're not the client."

Beryl changed the subject and attempted to put Morgan Ingram into a more talkative mood. "Those curved, two storey high panes are right out of a fantasy. They glisten in the sun! Do they expand and contract with heat and cold? How do you keep all the glass clean?" she asked.

"They're double paned and filled with argon gas... and mullioned in steel and rubber... well, synthetic rubber. My dad worked with a glass company to experiment with these expensive panes. Just one of them costs more than 90% of the houses in town. It was supposed to become a showplace for the glass company. He borrowed the money for the rest of the project. Fortunately, we've never had any trouble with leakage. The glass company also produced fiberglass and asbestos items that brought them a flood of lawsuits. The company went 'belly-up' years ago... another thing that broke my dad's heart. How do we clean them? Why... with great difficulty," he joked. "Actually, it's easy. We have a pressure hose that shoots water that's been loaded with a special detergent. It cleans the glass and then we have another solution we use to rinse it. It has the same ingredients that dishwashers use to eliminate spots. It softens the water, mostly. We squirt them every few months."

"And the interiors?"

"Same way... different hose. We move the furniture and rugs to the other side of the house. The curved glass goes two-thirds the way over to where it connects to the façade, but inside a glass partition goes up to meet it at the half-way point's zenith, directly overhead. The other side we wash the old fashioned way with long mops and scaffolding. Here, when we clean the insides, it's like standing in the rain. But there are drains at the bottom of the windows so the water washes the floors, too, before it rolls on out."

"Fascinating," Beryl noted. "Your dad must be very proud of the place."

"Yes, my father had intended to use the entire hilltop for a kind of intricate lawn, but he ran out of money. And then the troubles began."

"I'm intrigued," Beryl said. "What kind of trouble?"

Morgan laughed. "All kinds. It's been a mess. Like a Hydra. We solve one problem and create two more."

"Ah, yes," she laughed, "in the material world, that usually happens."

"Material world? Are you contrasting the material world with the illusory world? Perhaps as in *The Dancing Wu Li Masters?*"

"I guess I was. Sorry. I didn't mean to get all philosophical on you."

George cleared his throat. "When will your sister be available for conversation? We've come here from Philadelphia."

"Chloe told me that she met you yesterday. I know why you're here. There's no point trying to talk to her if she's not clear headed. So how's this? Would you two consider having breakfast somewhere with us tomorrow morning? I mean before she has anything to eat and drink here. It would have to be early."

"What time?" Beryl asked.

"Six."

"All right. We'll come by at 6 a.m.," George agreed.

"She's likely to look a mess. I thought my Aunt would solve that problem, but Chloe came back in the same condition she was in when she was driven to my aunt's place."

Beryl nodded. "Just get her dressed. After we pick you up, we'll go first to our motel. I'll put her in the tub, wash her hair and blow-dry it."

Morgan Ingram suddenly demurred. "She'll be too confused to dress herself, and I can't do it alone. Besides, her bedroom is next to Danvers' room. It would be much easier if I could just carry her out in her pajamas and slippers. Could you manage to get some clothing for her? I'll pay you for whatever it costs."

"Sure, I can do that. She looks to be about a size eight," Beryl agreed. "But put sneakers on her instead of slippers."

"Great. When you drive up don't park in front. Keep going until the house is out of view, and then wait. Everybody's gone from the other two houses so no one will see you. Don't sound the horn or anything. I'll come out with Chloe. Now, is there anything else I can tell you?"

George asked, "I have a few questions. Where can we reach your dad? And where is the yacht your mother and Pavano spend so much time on? It was in Philadelphia getting ready to sail. Is it still there? If it isn't, can you find out where it's bound?"

"My dad lives at the Y in town. Just call the desk and leave your number. They'll deliver the message for him to call you back. Give me your number, and I'll check on *The Shivadas'* location and call you with the specifics."

"I'd still like to know more about 'the troubles,'" Beryl said, sitting back in her chair.

"It's not a complicated story. There was a problem that my dad hadn't sufficiently solved. I can describe the problem with a line engineers like to use: 'It's easy to design a building that's a mile high. It's not so easy to get water up to the penthouse.' Drilling down to tap the aquifer was easy. What was hard was pumping the water up from below ground level to the top of this hill and keeping it under pressure.

"My dad planned to use windpower. It was quiet and cheap. He installed a wind turbine, but it didn't do the job. There were no electric lines anywhere around here in those days. The house requires no mechanical heating and cooling. My dad used velocity gradient for ventilation. The exhaust is in the dome. The wind blows over it and down the sloping house... we've got steps between each room. At the rear of the house there's a wide intake 'manifold' so the air circulates and vents in each room. A glass house functions like a greenhouse. On the rare occasions that additional heat is required, we have a small propane heater in the intake manifold. Anyway, back then he had one gasoline generator for the electricity we use to run appliances; he added another one for the water, and that did do the job."

"Then what were those 'troubles' he had?" Beryl asked.

"There were so many problems with producing the panes. One delay after another. We were living in an apartment in town, and the bills were piling up. He had to sell off some of the land up here. A developer built the two houses that are farther down the drive. There was an old dirt road that came up the back slope of the hill. The builder and the people he sold the houses to used that road. The steep road you came up was bulldozed by my dad. Later, he dedicated the road to the county and they paved it.

"The builder had helped himself to our water and power while construction was in progress. My dad intended to form little water and electric companies for all three homeowners to use. But my mom and dad were arguing like crazy at the time. There never was a formal agreement about water and power. When the divorce agreement gave my mother title to the property, she shut off their water and power. She didn't want them up here. Their kids would come and look in our windows. Anyway, when the utilities were cut off, they'd throw rocks at the glass.

"The people were apologetic and tried to make amends but my mother was unyielding. The developer disappeared. They solved the power problem with their own generators, and then the electric company decided to run a line up the dirt road. The owners had to have cisterns built to hold water that a big truck would come and fill every few weeks. It was a terrible way to live. The expense was enormous. The banks foreclosed.

"Bill Pavano and my mother operated an herbal supplement company; so for the convenience of their friends in the business, they bought the houses. She opened the water lines, but by then the water system was run by electricity. Ruth Danvers stayed in this house, my sister and I went to boarding school, and my mother and stepfather went around the world, conducting business or vacationing."

"So everybody lived happily ever after?" Beryl asked.

Morgan laughed. "Not quite. 'When I was a child, I spake as a child, I understood as a child, I thought as a child: but when I became a man, I put away childish things.' First Corinthians, 13:11."

"Did that King James' version hold true also for Chloe?" Beryl asked.

"Perhaps," Morgan said, smiling at Beryl's oblique 'Protestant' reference, "she should tell you that, herself. But don't ask her when Aunt Marietta is around, or Bill, either. He's also a very devout Catholic." He smiled.

"Are you planning to stay on here?" George asked.

"I'll be here for 'the duration,'" Morgan replied. "By that I mean for as long as it takes to get the estate settled. I just got my degree. I haven't accepted a position yet."

Beryl and George stood up to leave. As they walked back through the domed room, George complimented Morgan on the modern decoration. "It is a perfect fit for the house." He looked around. "There's nothing synthetic in here, is there?"

"Nothing. Everything is natural. Aside from steel and glass, it's slate, wool, silk, cotton, linen, leather, wood, or clay... hand woven, hand hewn, hand made."

"Who did the decoration? You or a professional?" he asked.

"Bill, actually. Funny, isn't it, how an asshole like that could have the taste to decorate my father's beautiful house."

Ross D'Angelo had waited in his office, hoping that George and Beryl would come by and tell him something that he could include in his report about the "possible remote control electronic beam." As George and Beryl entered the station, he jumped up from his chair and came to the front desk. "Let's go out for some dinner," he said. "My treat."

They walked to the corner of the block. "Take your pick," D'Angelo said, "Chinese? Italian? Mexican?"

"Which is the best?" Beryl asked.

"In my opinion? The Mexican. I don't like Chinese and being Italian, I tend to be exacting."

They went to the Mexican restaurant and ordered a margarita while they considered dinner.

Beryl saw her favorite dish on the menu: *Chicken mole.* "I don't eat meat often, but when I do..."

"Now she's the *Dos Equis* man," George teased, "of Margaritaville."

"Is she a mean drunk?" D'Angelo inquired, feigning serious concern.

"People send me sympathy cards," George laughed. "You should have seen her up at the Ingram House. Pavano was so goddamned snotty when he came to the door–"

"Snotty?" Beryl objected. "He told George the sight of his hand was offensive and advised him to wear a glove!"

"Jesus!" said D'Angelo, in genuine disgust. "I hope you decked him."

"She kicked the door and possibly dislocated his shoulder and gave the housekeeper a bloody nose."

"You're kidding!"

"No. No, I'm not." George laughed with the captain. "We didn't learn much today, not after all the commotion. All we really talked about was the history of the house, the problems with the water and power, and how to clean windows."

"Catherine Ingram was a spiteful woman. She casually destroyed those two families. They had been verbally misled and didn't understand the fine print. There was nobody to sue."

"So Morgan told us," Beryl said. "And then she reconnected the water lines when she bought the houses at a foreclosure sale. If it hadn't happened a dozen years ago I'd suspect the original owners of killing her."

"Lots of people were not unhappy to learn of her demise," D'Angelo confided. "She wasn't around much, but whenever she was, the Messenger of Heartache was likely to come knocking at your door."

"What happened with Dwight Ingram?"

"In her own way, she destroyed him professionally. We were typical kids in grade school, and then he took off intellectually. Summer school. Night school. He got a full scholarship to Columbia." D'Angelo had an idea. "How about if I call the Y and ask the desk clerk to deliver a message to Dwight, asking him to join us for dinner? You might as well meet the guy. This way, you'll have a proper introduction."

George was glad for the opportunity. "Sure, go ahead and call."

D'Angelo called the Y and left a message.

"Finish giving us some background info on him," Beryl said.

"He was the visionary type. Crazy about modern architecture. That man would talk about Frank Lloyd Wright the way golfers talk about Bobby Jones. A sacred kind of respect. Then he met Catherine and she was beautiful. So was her sister. They came to town and had all us guys hot and bothered. But they were super religious and we never figured it out. Catherine and Marietta. One went into a convent and the other married Dwight and clung to the insane idea that only if a woman intended to get pregnant could she have sex. She had two kids and then she moved her bed into the kids' room and left Dwight to sleep alone. No friends. Just church. Not even the Avon lady stopped at their apartment. Maybe Dwight thought he could win her back with that house... his crystal cathedral.

"With the help of a glass company and a lot of people who liked his visionary style, he bought the land and practically the whole face of the hill. He drilled a water well and put in a pumping station. It was all on private property then. Catherine hated the idea of having to go all the way down hill to buy a quart of milk or a dozen eggs. But she had her own room and he even designed a room to use as a chapel. It's on the backside of the house, where the entrance is. Behind one of those glass panes is a cut glass kind of panel that's configured in some geometric design... like the backdrop of a crystal altar. Next time you're up there get them to show it to you.

"His kids adored him but he was young and he was alone under all that stress. She just cut him out. He made his next big mistake by having an affair with his secretary. I guess you know the rest."

"When and where did Catherine start taking yoga lessons?" Beryl asked.

"Bill had opened *The Shivadas Center* in town not long after she had Chloe. My wife said that's where all the women went to get back into shape."

D'Angelo had finished just in time. The restaurant door opened and Dwight Ingram, looking like a college professor in a pale blue turtleneck sweater and brown tweed jacket, entered. The architect sat down to join them.

Beryl relaxed, listening to the three men talk about sports and agree on what they called "the fundamentals", describing themselves as "proud to be born at the time that Johnny Unitas' star had risen." "When you've been blessed like that at birth," Dwight said, "it's a kind of Biblical mark on your door. It gets you properly prepared for the advent of Joe Montana."

They ate chicken *mole* and fresh tortillas and finished off the meal with *flan*. Ross D'Angelo and George discovered that they had mutual friends in the New York City Police Department. As they began to talk "Cop Shop", Beryl announced that she had to go to Wal-Mart to get Chloe a change of clothing.

"Do me a favor," Dwight Ingram asked, "and let me come with you before these guys succumb to the urge to make an arrest for 'old time's sake.'"

"Yes," she laughed, "they are getting dangerously sentimental."

As they walked to the exit, Ingram called, "If we're not back in a couple of days, don't send a posse."

It was a pleasant October evening. Halloween decorations were in every store window. "Do you like living here?" Beryl asked as they walked.

"I used to dream about setting up practice in the Big Apple. Or maybe going out West. Arizona appealed to me. Taliesin West stuff. So did California. I really liked the Oracle Building. I've also had a secret love affair with the Kauffman place at Bear Run. I've never actually seen it - a million photos of it, sure - but never the real thing, face to face."

"I've seen it," Beryl said, "*Falling Water,* just southeast of Pittsburgh. We're from Philadelphia." She jokingly affected the attitude of a Chamber of Commerce booster. "The house is one of the Commonwealth's showplaces."

"And well it should be. Someday maybe you'll take me on the tour. What style architecture do you like?" he asked.

"I don't know enough about the subject to have a preference. But half of my apartment is decorated - that's the operative word - 'decorated' - in the old Japanese 'no nails' style of fitted joints. You might call it 'renovation natural.' I have a phony fountain and real goldfish in my meditation room. I once called it "faux Nipponese" and a Japanese lady I know corrected me, 'It's faux faux Nipponese.'"

Dwight Ingram laughed. "I'll have to remember that."

They entered the store and Beryl selected underwear, socks, and jeans. Then she asked him to select the shirt and jacket. If Chloe really likes them, I'll tell her you picked them out. If she doesn't, I'll take the rap." Beryl spent all of sixty-two dollars for the heiress's outfit. They laughed about the irony of it all as they returned to the restaurant in time to meet George and Ross who were just leaving. They said goodnight. Ross and Dwight went in one direction and Beryl and George went in another.

"Nice guy," Beryl said. "You can cross him off the Christmas list."

At the motel, they set their travel alarm clock. While they were watching TV, Morgan Ingram called with the details of the location of the yacht. George immediately called their associate Sensei Percy Wong in Philadelphia and asked him to learn all he could about the yacht and its occupants.

# WEDNESDAY, OCTOBER 26, 2011

At 5:45 a.m. Beryl drove the pickup truck up the hill and continued on until a curve in the road put them out of sight of Ingram House. She turned off the ignition. At 6:05 a.m. Morgan rushed up to the car, carrying his sister. They immediately drove down the long sloping back road and headed for the motel.

Chloe began to awaken in the chilled morning air. As George and Morgan watched television, Beryl shampooed Chloe's hair three times. When the young woman was fully awake, Beryl gave her a washcloth and told her to finish bathing, get dressed, and to holler if she needed help.

Beryl joined the men to watch the morning news. When Chloe emerged from the bathroom she bore no resemblance to the pathetic waif she resembled two days before.

Beryl blow-dried her hair and let her borrow some makeup. The two women had a mother-daughter look as they left to go out for breakfast.

"Tell us more about this drug regimen you're on," Beryl began the after-meal interview.

"I was supposed to see a specialist in Philadelphia, but for some reason my aunt had to get back. So we never did see a doctor. I had gotten a prescription for some heavy-duty tranquilizers when I got back in August. When that prescription ran out, Bill supplied me with more tranquilizers. Ever since my mother's death, I've preferred to be 'out of the mix.' This place has been crawling with their friends and business associates. It's a pleasure to sleep."

"Still, too much of that stuff may affect your brain. Why did you need 'heavy duty' tranquilizers in the first place?"

George and Morgan stopped talking to hear her answer.

"I was seeing a shrink before I got home," Chloe explained. "It had nothing to do with anything that happened here. I had been in Hawaii doing some work on volcanic gases and wanted to speak to a famous geology professor who was visiting from Cape Town. He left word that he'd see me that morning, but I was supposed to take a helicopter ride over Kilauea that morning. So I asked a friend who was also studying the volcano to switch helicopter trips with me. She did; but the pilot was inexperienced and set down in the wrong place. She jumped down and her feet got burned. I know it was the pain she was in, but she actually cursed me in front of dozens of people and said that if it weren't for me, she'd have been safe. I was shocked. She wouldn't even let me visit her. I sent her flowers but the nurse on duty told me she refused to look at them. They don't let flowers into the rooms of burn patients because of the bacteria in the water, but they do stand at the door and show the patients. She wouldn't even look at my flowers." Chloe's thoughts seemed to have been locked inside the incident. She stopped talking and stared at the table.

"Tell us about Miss Danvers."

"Oh, Danvers is not her name!" Chloe grinned. "It's Blackhawk. My aunt told you yesterday. My idiot stepfather thought that it was more elegant than her real name. She says she's Lakota Sioux. You'd think she'd be insulted by the name change, but they're thick as thieves. She dotes on Bill."

"Who hired her and when?" Beryl asked.

"She came just after Bill moved in. I've always supposed that he had known her and just asked her to come to work at our house."

"I can see the trouble you had in Hawaii causing you to get temporary emotional support from tranquilizers, but by October you surely were over it. You're allowing yourself to be drugged way beyond any therapeutic purpose. It can't be just to avoid socializing with others."

"Yes, it is. I didn't want to start trouble that I couldn't handle. You don't know how ruthless Bill can be. I didn't want to interact with him and Danvers at all. He'd put me in a mental hospital. Please don't think I'm kidding or exaggerating. Besides, if you really want to know the truth,

I was faking 90% of the time. I'd spit the pills out or deliberately puke them up. Then my Aunt came to see what she could do to restore my soul. She had business down in Philadelphia, and Morgan prevailed upon her to take me down there to see a specialist and hire an out-of-state private investigator, someone who wouldn't be influenced by Pavano."

"What was your Aunt's business there?" George asked.

"Something to do with the archdiocese. She had plans to start some kind of vocational school at the Haven. She thought that Bill wasn't going to come through with the money as he had promised. She wanted to see if there was any Church money available."

"I figured you were pretending to be semi-conscious," George said. "I saw how well you signed your name."

"Yes, the last thing I wanted was to have someone challenge the contract on grounds that I was not 'in command of my faculties.'"

Everyone grinned in agreement.

"Did you get to go with her into the rather impressive address of the archdiocese?" Beryl asked.

"No. She left me out in the rental car. I slept."

George asked, "Regarding the accident, is there someone you have in mind who acted as Pavano's accomplice?"

"No, just Danvers. I didn't intend to come home until Thanksgiving. I came home in late August because of the mess in Hawaii. Only Danvers was in the house. The other two houses were empty. My mother, Bill, and the rest of the Shivadas herd were supposed to return in ten days or so to get ready for Bill's big birthday party. I insisted that Danvers take a week off and go visit her 'old friends' back in South Dakota. I told her I had all these frequent flyer miles that she could use. I wanted my dad to spend a few days with me in our house. He still loves the place. I was starting to feel better about my friend's accident. My dad has a way of making a person feel better about nasty events. He's a wonderful man."

"And," Morgan interjected, "as soon as I heard that the two of them were going to be alone here, I caught the next flight in. It would have been nice to have the place to ourselves. But then Danvers decided not to go. The most we could hope for was to sneak dad into one of the rear houses and then come to the main house for a few hours when she went shopping. She had a lot of shopping to do for the party."

"Pavano and Danvers were in the house when the accident occurred. So, again," Beryl asked, "who could have acted as his accomplice? Who called from the base of the hill pretending to be you? Who ran your mom off the road?"

"How do we know that anyone called her?" Morgan protested. "We only know that Danvers said that someone called my mother and that my mother said that the caller was Chloe. And rather than being run off the road, my mother could have had someone in the car with her who whacked her on the head, swerved the car towards the edge, and jumped out. She wasn't going that fast. The car didn't have bucket seats. Anyone sitting beside her could have controlled the car... stepped on the brake... turned the wheel... slid out just before it went over."

"Ah," said George, "I didn't think of that. But someone did call from the bottom of the hill. Captain D'Angelo verified that on the gas station pay phone a call had been placed to Ingram House that evening at that precise time." George did not know this to be true, but in good police form he asserted as factual what was merely possible.

"So," Beryl countered, "your mother probably did get a call, but maybe she mentioned Chloe's name just as an easy excuse to leave the party." Morgan's theory, she thought, was childishly implausible. "There was no indication that anyone else had been in the car with your mother. There were no breaks in the skid marks, and the car doors were locked when the police arrived."

"So what happened next?" George asked Morgan.

"I looked around and noticed that I hadn't seen my mom for a while. I asked Danvers and she told me she had gone down the hill to help Chloe. I didn't know what to think. I had a rental car, so I drove down the hill and saw the skid marks. I looked over the edge and saw the car's headlights. The car never caught fire, so there was nothing to attract attention. I called 9-1-1. I saw my mother. She was dead. They had to use those 'Jaws of Life' to get her out."

"End of story," said Beryl.

Chloe dabbed her lips with the napkin. "I hope not. I want to know how and why Bill Pavano did it."

"One more question," Beryl said. "I know there was an age difference between your mom and Pavano, but what was the attraction? I've seen photos of your mom. She was a pretty woman. Why him?"

Morgan answered. "The mutual attraction was the mutual unattraction. According to rumor, my mother was as sexual as a bottle of sulfuric acid. And he was Italian, and if word had gotten out that he was in love with a blonde musclebound ski savant named Wes from across the lake in Vermont, he would have been ruined. His Italian relatives would not tolerate a homosexual on the family tree."

"Tell us about Wes."

"Dear Wes," Chloe sighed, "Wes Richter. His place is called *Shira Lodge*. *Shira* is the name of one of Kilimanjaro's three volcanic cones. He has ski instructors on staff, but he personally teaches special people. He taught me. I used to think it was because I was the first person who knew where the name *Shira* originated."

"Did you go too?" George asked Morgan.

"Before we went to college, all four of us would go. After that, there were no more ski weekends."

Chloe clarified the statement. "For the four of us they ended. Before I started college, I went through a period of depression and the three of us would go. Exercise was supposed to help. It was skiing as therapy."

"Did it help?" Beryl asked.

"I don't know. I don't know how I'd be feeling if I hadn't gone. Snow covers up what's underneath. Sooner or later it melts." Chloe pushed her teacup away. "Can we go back, now?" she asked.

Beryl and George began to feel at home in Ross D'Angelo's office. The police captain had never been stiff or formal with the two investigators; but now he was even more relaxed.

"What's the story about Danny and Chloe?" Beryl asked. "If the pay phone at the gas station was used, it's likely that Danny knows who made the call. Incidentally, George told Morgan and Chloe that you verified that a call had been made to the house from the pay phone there, at the time of the accident."

Ross D'Angelo smiled. "I did? That was good police work! I don't know what's going on between the two of them. I don't figure Danny for a liar. I asked if he had seen Chloe make a phone call on the night of the accident. He said, 'Don't involve me in anything that went on at that party. I'll tell you once. I didn't see Chloe make any phone call at the pay phone that night. Don't ask me again.'"

"What do you know about Marietta Post's 'Home for Unwed Mothers'?" George asked.

"I asked my wife and I now know that it's supposed to start teaching secretarial skills, and that it's located in a little town called Lizbeth near Cape Elizabeth, Maine. I know that it's named for a French saint, Therese of Lisieux. She was called, 'The Little Flower.'"

"Ah..." said George. "I know the one. She's always seen carrying a crucifix and a bunch of roses."

"Bingo," said Ross.

Before Sensei Percy Wong went down to the Maritime Office he stopped at his barber and had a manicurist trim and buff his nails. He intended to see about getting employed on the Shivadas in some culinary position, and he knew that his hands would be the first thing they noticed.

The harbor master's office told him where the yacht presently was docked as it received supplies from various chandlers. Dressed casually, Sensei walked along the wharf. He didn't imagine that the grandest vessel there would be the one he was looking for. A deliveryman had just left the ship. Sensei called to him.

"You want me?" the man looked around.

"Yeah, sorry to bother you. I see that you've just left the Shivadas. That is one impressive boat. I'm a little green about ships. What does a thing like that go for?"

"I don't know. Twenty million? They ain't cheap. Three tiers. Crew of twelve. I guess you can have a dozen 'guests' aboard. You ought to see the interior. Beautiful."

"What kind of people buy a ship like this... entertainers?"

"These folks don't entertain much. Or, if they do, they entertain Quakers. No champagne and no fancy scotch whiskey. The chef's Italian and they do drink good Italian wine. Lots of limes and quinine water and gin and vodka for the limes and tonic. But no vermouth... so there's no martinis. They're business people."

"I was hoping to get a job on one of these vessels. Culinary."

"They're lookin' for a bartender. You don't need to know a helluva lot about bartending cause, as I've said, they don't drink anything fancier than gin and tonic. You don't have to be much of a barman to know how to mix that."

"Thanks for the tip. I'll get right over to the maritime office and get my papers in order."

"Maybe you can catch the guy who just left. Kirby. I don't know his first name. He can fill you in on what to expect."

At the maritime office he saw a man carrying a duffle bag that had "Shivadas" printed on it. "I can't be this lucky," he said to himself. The man was in a long line waiting to sign out.

Sensei approached him. "Are you Kirby - just got off the Shivadas?"

"Yeah. I had to cut short my stint. My daughter's getting married."

"Congratulations. I was just talking to one of the guys who delivers food to the Shivadas. He mentioned that they're looking for a bartender. He said that maybe I could catch you to ask for some tips about working there. I'm culinary but he says the bartender doesn't have to be a 'mixologist' since they're not big drinkers."

"What did the guy look like?"

The question surprised Sensei. "Tall, ruddy complexion, blonde curly hair. He was leaving the ship about twenty minutes ago."

"Oh, Yeah. I know who he is. Nice guy but I don't know his name. Did you go aboard?"

"No. I met him on the dock. Great lookin' ship."

"It is that." Kirby seemed more relaxed.

"It's nearly noon. They're gonna slow down when people start going to lunch. You in a hurry?"

"No. Why?"

"You wanna go out for some lunch and a beer? My treat - for the info," Sensei said, maintaining a casual attitude. "You know a good place around here?" He had been holding his driver's license and his Transportation Worker Identification Credential in his hand. He took out his wallet and, making sure that Kirby could see what he was doing, he inserted the two cards into the wallet's slots. "I'm Percy Wong," Sensei said, extending his hand.

"Warren Kirby." He looked around. "Well... it's crowded in here today."

They went into a restaurant patronized by longshoremen. "The place looks like a dump," Kirby said, "but actually the food is pretty good."

"What's it like on the Shivadas?"

"Italian chef. Good food. I didn't particularly care for the people who owned it. They gave me the creeps. If you want my advice, find another ship."

"I'm strictly kitchen help," Sensei said. "But the delivery guy said I wouldn't need to know much about bartending if I signed on. He said they weren't big drinkers. Italian wine and gin and tonic."

"He's right about that. They don't need a bartender - which is why I had to do more food serving work than bartending. On a commercial cruise ship, you do exactly what you've been hired to do. But when you're part of a crew of a dozen or less, you have to share duties. But that didn't bother me. As I said, they're weird."

"How so?"

"You know when people are having a conversation and you approach them... carrying a tray of drinks or something... usually they keep on talking. The help is the help. Invisible. But not there. You bring the tray and when you're ten feet of them they stop talking, mid sentence. Then they wait until you serve them and if you're not quick enough, they look at you as if you're trying to eavesdrop on what they're saying."

"So you never really knew what they were talking about?" Sensei asked.

"I heard enough. They would talk about dead people and laugh. I know funeral jokes. A bartender knows all the jokes. But they laughed differently. There was something evil in it." He sighed. "I can't explain."

"I heard they were Italian. The delivery guy said they drank lots of good Italian wine."

"Yeah, most of them are Italian. Not the queen bee, Caterina. She's an American and doesn't speak Italian. And a guy from India, Gupta. Caterina and Gupta and her husband Bill spoke English to each other. There was a big guy there... overweight... ate enough for three people. They called him 'El Duce' or 'Il Principe.' Like he was a cardinal of the church. Cardinale his name was. He was the big boss. The Capo."

"Was he the queen bee's king bee?"

"He acted like it. But her husband was there. So he was always respectful towards her. He didn't speak English and she didn't speak Italian. Her husband spoke both languages."

"So what spooked you?"

"They would talk about getting publicity for what they were doing, but they wouldn't let you hear them talk about *what* they were doing. A few weeks ago we had a little problem with the icemaker so I was under the counter tryin' to fix it, and they didn't see me. Christ, I didn't know whether to stay hidden or get up and act like I hadn't heard anything."

"You got me interested. What the hell were they talking about?"

"About money and places we had stopped near, places that sounded like Keemasa, Cooloom, Emboco, Budbrum. And another place that sounded like the volcano in Hawaii, Kiluaka. But it was always death and disease. I knew the ship had something to do with charity, some mission of mercy. But why be so secretive about it?"

Sensei grinned and shrugged. "Yeah, that is weird. So what happened when you were under the counter?"

"They saw me and never treated me the same. When we got close to port I told them my daughter was getting married and asked to be relieved of my contract obligations. I forfeited a hunk of salary. But, like

I said, it gave me the creeps just being around them. Take my advice and find another ship."

"I was lookin' for a short stint. Just to be gone no more than a season. Maybe I'll rethink my options."

After they finished eating they walked back to the Maritime Office. Sensei went to the parking lot to get his car and Kirby went in to complete signing out of the ship's roster.

Sensei immediately called George and relayed all the information he had gotten. "What do you want me to do now?"

George reviewed the names and information he had recorded. He asked, "Is there any chance you could fly up to a place near Cape Elizabeth, Maine? It's just outside of Portland, on the coast. I'd like you to look over a Catholic home for unwed pregnant girls. It's called the *Little Flower's Haven*. They're supposed to be creating a new facility to train the girls for an office career or something. The woman who brought her over-tranquilized niece to our office is the director of the place. She was supposed to have come down to visit the archdiocese about something, maybe money for the project, maybe personnel, maybe something else. It's her sister's accidental death that we're up here investigating. It's a little too coincidental that she decided to come to Philadelphia at the same time that the *Shivadas* is docked there. Also, her sister Catherine was married to William Pavano of Philadelphia. Can you spare a few days to go up to Maine?"

"Just a few. I'll ask one of the regulars to cover for me at the Temple. I'm ok at the dojo. Maine? I'll probably have to hire a private plane. The *Shivadas* should be sailing any time now. The chandlers have been bringing food and supplies on board all day."

"When you get up to Cape Elizabeth find out if that yacht ever drops anchor anywhere nearby."

"Ok. I'll let you know what I find out."

Beryl didn't like the look on George's face. "How's Sensei getting on with the yacht surveillance?"

"He got to know a bartender who had just lied to get out of his work contract with them. The herbal business seems to have spooked him. Too many deaths associated with the ship's ports of call. He gave me the names of a few of the places. I'm gonna call Ted Cardone. He's in charge of policing harbor activities." George started to make the call. He hesitated. "Do you happen to know what 'Shivadas' means?"

"Devoted to Shiva."

George called Philadelphia Police Captain Ted Cardone, and after three tiers of screening, and an exchange of vital statistics and commentary on the changing world, Cardone asked, "So, old buddy, what can I do for you?"

"Is the port still your beat?"

"It is. And I long for the old days when vice walked the streets and hid out in abandoned houses. Now it comes in containers that cranes lift and in yachts with four bathrooms."

"A yacht is what I wanted to talk to you about. I'm investigating the death of one of the owners. My associate went down to the marina and talked to a guy who had just left his job on the ship... a bartender named Kirby. My guy's cover was as a job applicant. The bartender's advice: 'find another ship.' Let me kick around a few names with you."

"Go ahead."

"The yacht is a multimillion dollar ship called the *Shivadas,* which means, my partner assures me, 'Devoted to Shiva.' It's Panama registered and seems to serve as a floating corporate headquarters for a Sicilian-based herbal medicine distributor. Some of the names to look out for are Pavano and Gupta and another man from Sicily who is evidently very important. Cardinale. He's called 'Il Duce' or 'Il Principe' and is addressed as 'Your Grace' when they speak to him. He likes to eat. Other than that I have no information, except possible place names Keemasa, Cooloom, Emboko, Budburam, and Kiluaka."

The conversation ended like a dropped connection. The communication hadn't rolled to an end, running out of the energy of things to say. It just ended. George said, "Hello? Ted? Hello?"

Finally Cardone spoke. "George, I think that you should curtail your interest in this vessel and these people. What specifically got you interested in them in the first place?"

"We're investigating the death of William Pavano's wife, Catherine. She drove off a cliff. Her death was called an accident but her daughter thinks Pavano killed her. There is some ugly stuff going on. There's also a place called *The Little Flower's Haven* in Lizbeth, Maine, near Cape Elizabeth, that we're looking into. There's a connection but we're not entirely sure what it is."

"All I can tell you now is that I'll have to report this conversation. I'll vouch for you and ask if you can be brought into the loop. You know the feds. It ain't likely that they'll allow it. I'll call you and if I ask how the weather is, you'll know I can't talk about it. Meanwhile, be careful. Be very careful."

George relayed Cardone's warning to Beryl. "Let's get moving on this case. I'll go down to check out the Sicilian-blood boyfriend at the gas station."

Dan Brancati had just finished changing the oil of a vintage Porsche. "Nice, eh?" he said to George who was watching. "What can I do for you?"

"I'd like to ask you a few questions." George handed him his card. "I've been retained by Chloe Ingram to look into the circumstances of her mother's death. Do you recall the night of the accident?"

"Sure. I was on duty that night. We close up at 11 p.m."

"Someone called Ingram House from the pay phone outside. Did you see who it was?"

"No. If I had been anywhere out front I'd have noticed. I probably was working inside here on a car that was up on the lift. Sorry. I wish I could help."

"I understand that you and Chloe used to be close. She still speaks very highly of you. I know you're married and I'm not trying to compromise you. But can you give me your opinion about what she's going through up there in Ingram House. Have you seen her lately?"

"I'll tell you the truth. I saw her pass in a car with her Aunt Marietta. She looked like hell. Half dead. Are they keeping her drugged?"

"Evidently. When's the last time you talked to her and she was alert, sober, drug free?"

Brancati did not answer the question. "The week she got home from Hawaii, she was very upset."

"About what?"

"About something that happened there. Something about a geologist from Cape Town University freaked her out. She didn't tell me what it was. But it really bothered her because she came home a couple of months early."

"Was she taking medications then?"

"She asked me for some Valium I had. I told her to see the doctor here."

"And she told you nothing about the 'thing' that happened in Hawaii?"

"No. Nothing. I thought it was some geological problem, but Chloe didn't want to talk about it."

"Are you sure you're telling me everything? I'd like to think I can trust you. Her life is in danger."

Dan Brancati looked away. He stared out the window, trying to reach a decision. "If I hadn't seen her for myself, I'd never break the promise. I told her I'd never mention this to anyone, but, all right.

"She wanted me to help her search the other two houses up there... for drugs, I guess. Nobody was staying in them at the time. She wanted to break in, well, not exactly break in, since she had keys. I went with her the first time she entered. We didn't find anything. The housekeeper started to come back to the house so we slipped out the back door and came back to the gas station via the back road. The next day she dropped a paper bag off here. She put a note on it: 'Hold this for me. Guard it with your life.'"

"Where is it?"

"It's up on the shelf in the supply cabinet."

"Could I, at least, take a look at it?"

Brancati laughed as he left the room. "It isn't what you think it is." When he returned, he carried a small brown paper bag that had a rubber band around it. He handed the bag to George. "This is it. I threw the note away."

"Did you look inside?"

"Sure. It's three boxed bottles of Viagra. I thought it was a joke. I called her but Mrs. Danvers said she was 'indisposed.' I haven talked to her since. Take it. There's no point in my keeping it now."

"Ok, Dan. I appreciate it."

George returned to the motel and tossed the bag on Beryl's bed. She pulled off the rubber band, opened the bag and looked inside it. Feigning delight she cooed, "Darling, I thought this was to be a working weekend!"

George threw a pillow at her. "I hate it when a client lies to me. What time is it now in Cape Town, South Africa?"

Beryl consulted her iPhone. "They're six hours ahead of us. Don't ask me about Daylight Saving Time."

"Tomorrow morning let's get up early and talk to the geology professors of Cape Town University and see which one went to Hawaii recently and find out if he talked to Chloe Ingram. I think that story about her friend getting burned was pure bullshit. But let's prove it. She was here in September so the accident would have had to have happened in July or August. It was supposed to involve a helicopter service at Kilauea. How many helicopter services are there? We're six hours ahead of Hawaii. Let's start making calls to see if one of the pilots knows about a burn accident this past summer."

Beryl looked at the boxes that contained the plastic bottles of pills. "First, what about these? If Ted Cardone doesn't want to talk about the problem, you can bet that these people are selling fake drugs. This is an international criminal problem. We may be sticking our noses into a beehive."

"I know. I know. Ayurvedic medicine makes a great cover for an illegal pharmaceutical enterprise. Most of these fake drugs come out of Asia. And the Sicilian mafia distributes them."

"It's important to get our ducks in a row. Let's see if we can determine that these supplies of Viagra are phony. We could send them to a lab and wait on the results, and by doing that tip off a lot of people, or, you could make an appointment with a doctor here and ask for help with your erectile dysfunction and then go to the drug store," she began to shake, trying to suppress the urge to laugh, "and get the prescription filled locally so that we can compare the pills and the boxes on our own. If they're different, we'll be on more solid ground when we raise the suspicion."

George was offended. "I do not have erectile dysfunction! How can I go to a doctor and fake it?"

Beryl could no longer control the urge to laugh. She giggled mischievously. "George, he's not going to show you porn and see what you can come up with. He's not gonna test you."

"How the hell do you know what he'll do? I'm not going to have some quack poke around my perfectly good junk and maybe louse it up just looking for a non-existent problem."

"I could go and say I'm going for a needy friend," Beryl teased. "I guess erectile dysfunction doctors hear that line a lot. Usually, though, it's a *guy* who has 'a needy friend.' Maybe I could go in drag."

George threw his second pillow at her and laughed. "The Shivadas is getting ready to sail. My guess is that the Atlantic is the perfect place to cure a bee-stung nose with that old salt-water panacea. Let's not plan to spend any time 'walking the plank.' Ok. I'll call the doctor in the morning. I'll just pray it's not a lady doctor." He waited for Beryl to say something "smart-assed."

"Don't look at me," she said. "Regrettably, I have no basis to form an opinion in the matter. It's one of the tragedies of my life."

They called all of the helicopter services that flew over the Kilauea volcano. There had been no accidents involving burns.

# THURSDAY, OCTOBER 27, 2011

Before breakfast, George called the Geology department of the University of Cape Town and asked the receptionist if the professor who had recently been to Hawaii had returned yet.

"Yes," she said. "That would be Professor Boorman. I just saw him pass my door. He should be in his office. Do you want me to connect you?" George said yes and wondered if his luck would continue.

"Who is this calling?" the Professor asked.

"My name is Wagner. I'm a private investigator. I've been retained by a young lady you met in Honolulu recently, Miss Chloe Ingram. I've learned about a conversation you had with her and I was wondering--"

The professor was both blunt and reasonable. "If you want to know about a conversation I allegedly had with your client, why don't you ask your client? I regard your call as an unwarranted intrusion into my privacy. It is harassment, and if you call me again, I will make a formal complaint about your activities." He disconnected the call.

"All I have accomplished," George said, "is to ruin the day of what is probably a very nice man."

In the motel's information pamphlet, George found a physician whose specialty was Urology. Since his first name was Anthony, George called.

Doctor Anthony Derr's office nurse was encouraging. "The tourist season's over," she said. "You can pretty much pick your time."

George said he'd be there after breakfast if that was agreeable. "Shall we say at 10 a.m.?" the nurse asked.

"Yes," said George. "I'll see you then."

Beryl checked the boxes. "They contain thirty pills each. Make sure you tell him that you want a month's supply. And also be sure to mention that a friend of yours gave you a few pills to try and you took them and they worked fine and you had no side effects whatsoever. He may not want to turn a stud like you loose with a revamped 'rocket in your pocket.'"

George got ready for the appointment. "*Oh, the humanity!*" he called from the shower.

Beryl looked at the list of names Kirby, Sensei's "informant," had given him. The names sounded African and Cape Town was in South Africa. She had an acquaintance who was a member of the Togolese delegation to the U.N. She looked up the number, called, and left a voicemail message, asking to be called back.

Sensei engaged a private airplane at an executive airport to take him - on a one-way basis - to Portland, Maine. The pilot, a middle-aged retired Navy aviator, boasted that his 1986 Piper Archer, which he used daily in his "specialized" service to New England, maintained its perfect condition because he used only heated hangars during winter months. "I'll land anyplace, providing I can berth it in a nearby heated facility. And the rest of the year, I insist on keeping it inside. I never leave it out in the open. In an emergency I use a heated snood for the engine."

"It makes sense," Sensei concurred. "Do you get much traffic on this run to Portland?"

"More than you think. It's spotty, though. Because I've really winterized the aircraft, I'll fly up here in any weather. A lot of guys won't. People don't like the hassle of big airports, although up here, other than Boston's, the terminals are all small. Sometimes people want privacy. A private plane, by definition, is private. I just had a lady with a sickly younger woman who flew down and back from Southern Maine. Portland. The girl was so out of it she'd never be allowed to get on a big commercial aircraft."

Sensei suspected that the two women were the client and her aunt. "Did you take them down and back from Portland? Can you do that in one day?"

"These two, yes. It was one day. Portland's got a heated terminal, but today I've got a special customer I've got to pick up in Bangor. An old Captain of mine. He likes to play golf year round. I take him everywhere there's a senior player's tournament."

"Ah, so that's why I could only get you for one-way. Do you specialize only in New England?"

"No, northern New York... the lakes' mostly. And all the ski resorts in season. In the summer there's lots of traffic to those old ritzy 'summer houses' that were built before air conditioning came along. I have quite a few 'regulars.'"

"You're like a private chauffeur. That's neat. Do you have many regularly scheduled runs?"

"Mostly, I have preferential clients. Recently, for example, I've been real busy with a big birthday party they had over in Lake George. I've been taking people back and forth. Then there was a funeral and the usual lawyer's meetings. I've got a few more flights booked. These particular clients tip well so I give 'em service any time of day or night. Their base in Philly is a yacht. So, since yachts don't have garages, I provide any out-of-town transportation. If it's humanly possible, I take 'em wherever they want to go. How long you plannin' on staying at Lizbeth?"

"Until I get a few answers to a few questions. A few hours, no more. I was looking at a map back in the airfield and I see that I'm on the same latitude as Lake George. A couple of my associates are there. I could maybe drive back to Philly with them. How hard is it to get a private flight to Lake George?"

"I can't take you because of my Bangor pickup. But let me call a good pilot I know in Portland. You can take the same bus back from Lizbeth, but if I'm not mistaken, that last bus leaves around noon. You want me to book him if he's available?"

"Sure," Sensei said. "I'll be finished by then and be back in Portland to meet up with him."

The pilot flicked through his iPhone and placed the call. After speaking to the pilot, he turned to Sensei, "He's got a fare going into Glens Falls to pick up another passenger. He can take you there. It's just a few miles south of Lake George with a good highway between."

"What's his e.t.a.?"

"3 p.m."

"Tell him he's got a date." Sensei waited until the pilot disconnected his call and then he called Beryl to give her the estimated time of arrival in Glens Falls.

The bus to Lizbeth had just departed when Sensei arrived at the bus station. He hailed a cab, and drove out to the seaside community.

"You get much traffic out to Lizbeth?" he asked the driver.

"Ay-ah."

"Did you ever hear of a Catholic institution there... The Little Flower Home?"

"Ay-ah."

"Good. Then can you drive me right to it?" Sensei took a deep breath and waited to hear the response.

"Ay-ah."

Sensei had no further questions and looked at the town from the road as they passed it and went on to the institution. The cab parked at the gate. The driver stopped the meter and held his hand out to be paid. "We's he-ah. Can't git any closah."

The fare was clearly visible and needed no further conversation to pay. Sensei gave him a generous tip and asked him to wait while he got out of the cab and peered through the wrought iron gate.

The building reminded him of one of those English manors, a place where they chased foxes. There were women out on the lawn, getting sun... but because of their voluminous habits, he could only see their faces. He could not even swear that, given their garments, they were all women. Many seemed to be walking like zombies... slow and deliberate. Some women were old and required assistance when walking. Some were young. He could not tell if any of the young ones were pregnant. But there were others who didn't seem old or sick or drugged into a zombie state at all. Many of them sat in small groups, having animated conversations... laughing... gabbing... entertaining each other by imitating the way certain people danced or walked. He got back into the cab. "Can you see the ocean from anyplace nearby?" he asked, knowing that he'd get the same apparently affirmative answer.

This time the "Ay-ah" response seemed to have a suspicious tone. Sensei felt a sense of xenophobia - not the simple ethnic or racial desire of a group to expel the "not of this body" stranger, but rather the muted suspicion that the newcomer was there to steal from the locals, to jeopardize their way of living or set in motion an alien way of life. The cab driver pushed up the meter flag, starting a new fare.

They drove for fifteen minutes and then the cabbie parked in a small area at which the road bifurcated. One sign, "Bride's Tor," pointed to a path that led up through granite boulders to a cliff. Sensei had the strange fear that if he chose that path he'd climb up and look down to see both the ocean and the tail lights of the cab as it departed.

The other sign said, "Beach lookout." Sensei started down that path, turning back to remind the driver that he'd be only a few minutes. As he began to jog, the path turned sharply, separating as it did, what had only been landscape to what was now only seascape. His footsteps disturbed what seemed to be hundreds of white birds that were nestled in the rocks and clumps of sedge grass. The wide-winged birds suddenly began to flap their wings frantically in an effort to become airborne, surrounding Sensei in what seemed to be a wild pillow feather fight. Sensei laughed, waiting for the view to clear so that he could inspect the little bay area and judge if a yacht could drop anchor there.

The path ended at a small wooden staircase that went down into the ring of coarse yellow-brown sand that formed the beach. He could feel the spray of the waves that crashed against the rocks jutting out into the water; and though he searched the horizon, there was no sign of ship or human habitation anywhere, not even a jetty or a shack. There was just the violent ocean made blue by the sky, the ring of ecru sand, black granite rocks, white sea foam and birds, and the sounds of the wind, the mewing cries of the gulls, and the thunderous waves. Yes, he thought, if a ship had a motorized craft aboard, it could lower it into the water and take people or cargo at least close to the beach. It would have to have a motor. He had once seen a large ship lower a motorized boat to take people into a dangerous shoreline. The boat dropped anchor, and the people transferred to a dinghy which was tethered to the boat; and once the waves carried them safely onto the strand, the dinghy was manually pulled back to the boat which then hoisted its anchor, started its engine, and returned to the mother ship. Without an arrangement such as this, no dinghy could have been launched into those waves and made it back.

He returned to the cab, surprised that it was still waiting. "How do the ships pickup and deliver cargo to the beach?" he asked.

"A row boat can come in, but it takes a lot of hoss-powah ta git back out."

"That's what I figured," Sensei replied. "Can we go into Lizbeth now?"

"Ay-ah."

In Portland, just as Sensei prepared to board the private plane, he checked again with Beryl. He related the oddities of his journey. "By a weird coincidence, the flight I got to Maine seems to have been the same plane that Ms. Post and the Ingram girl took to get down to Philadelphia. He said he took others to a party and then to a funeral. They seem to be 'favored' clientele. Big tippers. They could be our yacht dwellers." Then he described the beach and the apparently affirmative response he got when he asked if ships dropped off people and cargo at the beach. Then he related the even odder information he had obtained in Lizbeth.

"I went back to town and figured that the people who would know anything were the food purveyors. I went to the only bakery in town and praised the 'good work' that's being done at Little Flower. I said that I had heard that the nuns out there were particularly appreciative of the high quality of their baked goods. The owner says - now forgive me if I attempt to imitate the accent - 'They-ahs one thing we know for show-ah in this world. If we live long enough, we'ah gonna git old. We don't know what condition ow-ah minds and bodies will be in ow-ah wanin' yee-ahs.'

I said, 'Amen.' Then she says, 'It's comfortin' to know that the Church just doesn't discaad ya when ya can't do ya' job.' So I picked up on this and said, 'And judging from the quality of the food they receive, they not only don't discard you, they honor your service.' She said that they had a rich benefactor and insisted I eat one of the cherry tortes she had just made for them. I know fresh cherries when I taste them. Quality stuff.

"I took my suspicion to the bus station. I asked, 'Do you still have young women who need help coming here?' He says, 'Do ya mean pregnant girls who go out to Little Flah-wah?' I say, 'Yes. I heard that's where they went.' He says, 'Mistah, that is old news ya got. It's been thirty yee-ahs since anybody used that place for unwed mothahs. Tain't even church propity no maw.' I asked, 'It is exclusively for retired nuns?' And he makes a gesture - he points to his ear and makes circles with his finger. He meant that some were mentally ill."

"That's weird. A secular home for nuns? Using unwed mothers as a cover for the mentally ill? This case is getting stranger by the hour. What's remarkable is the way that Marietta Post lied about it. She created an elaborate training program for these young women that she says was introduced by the guy she's accusing of killing her sister. And it's all baloney! So is there any bad news?"

"You're gonna get one hell of a bill for the planes I chartered. And you'll have to drive down to Glens Falls to pick me up at 3 p.m."

"It'll be worth it. The job is presenting dangers we hadn't anticipated. We'll pick you up at the airport at three."

At one o'clock George returned from his visit to the doctor and his visit to the local pharmacy. "No appointment necessary? My ass. There were two old guys ahead of me. I am warning you. Do not make jokes about this."

Beryl had planned to make several teasing remarks. She mentally censored them. Knowing George, she knew that he would deliberately relate the events in a way that was designed to make her laugh and that he would laugh, too. "First," she said, "Sensei called. We have to pick him up in Glens Falls at 3 p.m. He's flying from Portland. We'll drive home together. Oh, he says it isn't a home for unwed mothers. It's probably a home for nuns who've got mental illness-but he saw other people of various ages milling around that didn't appear sick. Women, maybe even men. It's not official Church property anymore, so God knows what the place is being used for."

"You know," George said, "I figured that 'unwed mother' haven was a lot of bull, but I'm relieved. I was starting to worry that they were involved with some baby-selling business. All those byzantine lies!"

He recited the morning's events and lamented his sufferings at the hands of "Doctor Feel Good." Finally, they settled down to examine the boxes and the contents. Sitting by the window to get the natural light, they examined and compared the two boxes and their contents.

There was no doubt. The boxes were different. The cardboard was of different quality and the box bottoms and tops had been folded by a different mechanical process. The printing was the same style and font size, but the colors had different shades. The product information sheet inside the phony box was a sloppy photocopy. The margins were uneven and the printing was blurred in places. The packaging of the pill bottle, the security seal, and the pills, themselves, showed subtle, but detectable, differences.

"The feds have to conduct the lab analyses. We're finished when we turn the stuff in," George said.

"How do you propose to turn them over to the feds without involving Dan and Chloe? She should be the one to give them to the authorities. Her testimony is necessary to establish provenance."

"The evidentiary chain has already been broken," George countered. "What difference does it make?"

"To the young husband and father who was doing our client a favor, it means a lot. He entered the premises with her. He already has enough marital problems. His wife may wonder just what he was doing with Chloe in the first place. Why ruin his life? Besides, the deaths that Kirby the bartender talked about didn't come from phony Viagra."

"I know. We need to get the lethal stuff. It could be AIDS medications or chemotherapy or penicillin. Phony Viagra isn't going to arouse much official indignation. Interpol will probably know what's going on in the international phony drug trade."

Beryl teased, "What will you do with the real pills? Give them to the guys down at the precinct for Christmas presents? Go ahead! Be a hero!"

George jumped on the bed and gave her head a Dutch rub. They were laughing when the phone rang. George answered, clearing his throat and suppressing a final hiccough laugh. Ted Cardone was calling.

George recognized his voice. "What's up, Ted?"

"You asked me if anything was new on the Delaware River. We found a floater this morning."

"Shit! Who?"

"A bartender from one of the ships. Warren Kirby of Trenton, New Jersey. How's the weather up there, George?"

"Overcast. It's really clouding in."

Anais Febre, of Togo's U.N. delegation, returned Beryl's call.

Beryl asked, "Let me run some names by you. I think they're place names, probably African. I don't have the correct pronunciation or spelling, so you'll have to use your imagination." She opened her little blue tablet. "Keemasa, Coolom, Emboko, Budbrum, Kiluaka. Do these names mean anything to you?"

Anais did not hesitate. "They're locations of refugee camps."

"Have you heard any scandals about people dying because of phony medicine at these camps?"

"Ah, Beryl. There are outbreaks of disease at every refugee camp. The mortality rate is abysmal. People don't enter a refugee camp the way they enter a resort hotel. The refugees are starving to begin with. They're exhausted and haven't had any medical care in months or years. The sanitation at the camps is terrible. A wave of disease might engulf hundreds at a time. Sometimes a medicine is supposed to be refrigerated; and they just don't have refrigeration. Sometimes they give the patient a supply of pills, and the patient sells them. He or she will never admit this, and when there's no improvement, the doctor blames the medicine.

Newspapers blame the doctors and the warlords. There are so many opportunities for fraud and incompetency."

"What's your take on the phony medicine possibilities?"

"I have no doubt that there's a big trade in bad drugs. I know of one case in which vials of water were sold as vials of tetracycline. The patient could hardly be blamed for selling the medicine. The injection was completely ineffective. But with tablets and capsules, proving it can be difficult. You'd have to go through the officials of the host country, and they're the ones who share in the profits from the scam. Don't make enemies. The racketeers are a ruthless bunch."

"In that case I won't involve you further by saying another word about it. So how are things in Togo?"

As they drove north to Lake George, Sensei related his experiences. Before he finished, George's phone rang. Morgan Ingram was calling.

"Has anyone associated with Wagner and Tilson," Morgan asked, "been up to Maine recently?"

"Yes," George answered, "this morning. Our associate checked out Little Flower's Haven."

"My aunt just called. She said you had no authority to snoop around her institution and interrogate the neighbors. I didn't want to antagonize her any more than she already was, so I just said that I didn't know the parameters of the agreement."

"It didn't take long for the news to get to her. Why would a few innocuous questions upset her so much?"

"I don't know why. You've met her. She's not the warm and fuzzy type. I have never even seen the place. My father calls it, 'The Manhattan Project.' Top secret. Are you at the motel?"

"No, we're on the road back from Glens Falls. We've just picked up our number three guy, Sensei Percy Wong, the one who did the snooping."

"Is he the one who taught Beryl all those karate moves?"

"Yes, he is. He's also a Zen Buddhist Priest."

"I'd like to meet him."

"How about an early dinner tonight?"

"At Rosarita's?"

"Sounds good to me. Can you invite your father and sister and Ross D'Angelo?"

"I just saw Chloe. She's half-asleep. But I'll call Ross and my dad. We'll meet you at the restaurant around 4:30 p.m. How's that?

"We'll be there. Maybe we can have breakfast again with Chloe tomorrow morning, early."

"Sounds good to me. Same time. Same place."

The circular family tables at Rosarita's seated six people; and by 4:30 p.m. all of the seats at one table were taken. Beryl, George, Sensei, Ross, Dwight Ingram and Morgan Ingram all ordered the house specialty, chicken *mole*.

George spoke with his authoritative voice. "Some aspects of this case are beyond the scope of our investigation. So, unless a subject has something to do with the death of Catherine Pavano, we non-official investigators can't get involved."

"How do you know where to draw the line?" Ross D'Angelo reasonably asked. "Mrs. Pavano had an active business life; and unless you're prepared to dismiss her business associates from the list of suspects, you've pared down the list to an impossible few."

"I'm not ready to cross anybody off the list," George said, "but I don't think we have to probe that far into the Shivadas business. If the company has criminal dealings, the appropriate law enforcement agencies will handle it."

"George," Ross gently protested, "I'm with one of those appropriate agencies. This is a death in my jurisdiction and a lot of those people were within fifty yards of the accident or crime. This may not be the best time to tell you, but I called Interpol and was put in touch with a guy in the UN High Commissioner for Refugees' office. Shivadas may be more involved in Catherine's death than we figure."

"And if it is," Beryl said, "that places the case outside our boundaries. I think I can safely say that after we've eliminated all of the suspects who are not in Shivadas, we're gonna consider our work done. If that means that we haven't fulfilled our contract, so be it. We'll refund our client's money."

"I thought your contract required you to prove that Bill Pavano killed my mother," Morgan protested.

"Only if he's guilty," Beryl retorted.

Ross D'Angelo regretted bringing up the U.N. contact while possible suspects were present. He quickly changed the subject. "On another point of interest, after we discussed verifying the phone calls that were made from the gas station, I checked and found that *two* calls were made from the gas station to your house that night: the call that Catherine got and another one at 11:20 p.m."

"I didn't talk to anybody," Morgan said. "I went with my mother's body to the morgue."

"Could Chloe have taken the call?" Ross asked simply.

"She wasn't home!" Morgan said emphatically. "She could not have taken any call - not on a land line anyway!"

"Oh, sorry. I wasn't thinking," the captain apologized. "I wasn't trying to trap you. I really did forget that."

Morgan grunted. "We just get deeper in bullshit. My sister is suffering!"

"I think I know who made the call," Dwight Ingram interjected. "It was Wes." Everyone looked surprised.

"That's good news! We're getting somewhere!" D'Angelo slapped the table. "How do you know?"

"One of the men at the Y heard that there was an accident at Ingram House, and that a woman had been taken to the morgue. I was worried that it was Chloe, but I didn't want to call the morgue to ask if the female they had on a slab happened to be my daughter. I'm her father. I shouldn't have to go around asking for news. So I walked over to the house. Wes Richter was standing at the gas station looking up at the hill. The station was closed, but he was under a street light by the pay phone. It was around 11:30. I didn't have my watch on."

"Did you talk to him?" George asked.

"No. I didn't let him see me, either. There was a police car at the base of the hill. I watched and then a guy I know walked by and told me that it was Catherine who died in the crash."

Beryl looked surprised. "Why didn't you mention this before? Didn't you find it strange that a man would be standing there at that time?"

"No. Not at all. I've known about Wes and Bill Pavano for a long time. So did Catherine. She knew it before she married him. To my ex-wife, my *first* ex-wife, a eunuch would have been the perfect husband. But they are difficult to find. A homosexual male would have been her second choice."

"I'll second that," Morgan nodded. "I wasn't around the two of them that much, but my mother and Bill slept in separate bedrooms, and Wes would sneak in to be with Bill. He liked the privacy of Ingram House."

Sensei asked, "If your mother knew they were lovers, and she didn't object, why did they have to sneak around? Couldn't they come 'out'?"

"No," Morgan said. "Not flagrantly, anyway. And certainly not when the Sicilian bosses were at the house. There were other reasons, too, why discretion was absolutely necessary. Shira Lodge became a success because a bunch of sex-starved matrons brought their families there. Wes was the secret love of the righteous! Ironical. He'd play those women for all they were worth; and they all believed him when he said that his respect for them, their families, and their Christian values kept him from nailing them right there on the slopes."

Ingram laughed. "You forget the ski pants. The damn things prevented him from ravishing so many of New England's purest crab cakes."

Morgan returned to the evening pay-phone call. "That's why Wes always called to make sure before he drove up. And also why he used that pay phone. They didn't like to leave evidence around by way of personal phone bills. The people associated with the herbal business would drop in with their friends whenever they wanted. The two rear houses were bought specifically for their use. One guy is Italian nobility. He bought into their business about ten years ago. He started out as a thin guy, good looking. He fell in love with my mother. Big mistake. He gained two hundred pounds. Loving her must have required comfort food. He thought my mother was a saint." Morgan began to laugh in a sardonic way that indicated that it was an "inside joke" to which the others were not privy. "One time he met Wes in the main house. He thought that Wes was his competition for my mom's love. Poor Wes. He was almost killed because someone suspected him of being heterosexual."

Everyone laughed. Beryl asked, "What happened when there were people up there?"

"Then Bill would go down to meet Wes. Chloe told me that Mom would send him to the store to give him an excuse."

"Jesus!" George said. "That's one hell of a family dynamic."

Sensei had a question: "When and where was Chloe when she learned of her mother's death?"

Morgan answered. "She left for one of the lakes up in Hamilton County. Lake Lila, to be exact. It's in the middle of nowhere. As the crow flies, it's only 75 or 100 miles from here. She called me when she got there. I was worried. Since she got home from Hawaii, she'd been a nervous wreck."

Dwight Ingram amplified the assessment. "I've never seen her so torn up. She came to me as soon as she got home. She wanted me to stay with her in the house. But Danvers wouldn't go away, so we had to spend time hiding in the two houses. She didn't want her mother to know she was seeing me. I think it comforted Catherine to believe that her children thought I was some kind of monster."

"Anyway," Morgan resumed, "after a few weeks she began to pull herself together. Danny Brancati down at the gas station helped to calm her. I admit it. I was afraid that in her condition she'd fall crazy in love with him again, so I suggested she do some research up in the mountains for a week around the night of the party. She didn't want to be here for the festivities."

Sensei repeated the question. "When and where was she when she learned of her mother's death?"

Morgan responded indignantly. He took out his phone and flicked through some logs. "Here," he said to Sensei, "is the text message she sent me on Sunday, October 2nd, at 7 a.m. You can read it for yourself."

"That's not necessary," Sensei said.

"No! Please. Then let me read it for you! It says in abbreviated words, 'Hi Morg, hope you survived birthday bash. Got some good samples. Fossils too. Is it safe to come home? Text me if they're staying on. Else I'll see you at 1 or 2 p.m. Love Chloe.'" He shoved the phone across the table. "Read my reply."

Sensei read, "Chloe, I'm on the road up to North Creek. Can you meet me at the Inn there?"

"Why didn't you just call her back?" Beryl asked.

"Because my phone was off!" Morgan chafed at being questioned. "I didn't get the message until noon. I had just awakened. I was with the police until dawn. Think about it! Chloe was just getting her shit together. At noon she'd be on the highway heading home. Should I call her while she's driving and say, 'Mom is dead'? I met her at the Inn and told her there. Just to be certain, I asked her if she had called the house the night before. She said, 'No.' I didn't want Chloe to walk into our crazy house alone. There were still guests there and people who believed that she had called from the base of the hill. So I drove up and met her halfway at North Creek. Before we headed back, I called Danvers to be sure the guests were gone."

Sensei returned the phone to Morgan. "How did you find out about your mother's accident?" he asked.

"Where and when?" Morgan Ingram seemed to find the question amusing. He paused to look at George quizzically. "Were you expecting my answer to change? Do you three not talk to each other? Why is it necessary for me to be interrogated by another one of your cohorts, sitting around a dinner table with my father?"

Sensei responded immediately. "The error is mine, and I apologize for it. The drive up from Glens Falls was much shorter than I expected it to be. I didn't get to discuss the case as I'd hoped. I'm sorry. I didn't mean to antagonize you."

Everyone seemed satisfied, yet Morgan's response had ended all conversation. Beryl prepared to leave. "Is tomorrow morning at six still a good time to get Chloe?" she asked Morgan.

"Yes, I'll have her ready."

Beryl asked, "Maybe your father would enjoy having breakfast with us."

"Why?" Morgan asked. "So that you can include him in the audience when you try to make me look like I'm hiding something?"

Dwight Ingram stood up. "I'd enjoy having breakfast with all of you tomorrow." He put his hand on Beryl's arm, bent down and whispered, "If you're not busy right now, I'd like to show you the only other house I've designed. The owners are away, and the real estate agent gave me the key for today." He turned to Morgan. "There was no need to be rude. I'd appreciate it if you'd apologize to Miss Tilson and to Mr. Wong."

"I'm not a child, Dad. I don't need to be reprimanded."

"I'm asking you to apologize."

Morgan relented. "All right. I shouldn't have been so curt. I was rude and I do apologize. But we're all a little tired of getting no place fast. First there's an assault and battery at the front door, then trouble at Little Flower's Haven. Now it's this repetitive questioning of the victims."

"What happened at the front door?" Ingram asked.

"Miss Tilson nearly broke Danvers' nose and dislocated Pavano's shoulder," Morgan explained.

Dwight Ingram pretended to be confused. He looked quizzically at Beryl. "Is that included in your fee or do we have to pay extra?" He turned to Morgan. "Since when would that be considered a bad thing? And stirring up trouble at the 'Spa for the Spiritually Wishful'? Can that be bad? Son, causing trouble for that 'money pit' is a noble endeavor." He guided Beryl to the door, turned and jingled some keys for Ross D'Angelo to see. He whispered to Beryl, "I'll give you the chance to make alterations in my plans. Since you're attired like a proper Buddhist 'biker chick' - wearing wool, not leather, I'll take you on Ross's motorcycle. I have an extra helmet."

"How far away is this house?"

"Five miles, but the road is good. I asked Ross to detach the sidecar. I didn't think you'd want to look like a cupcake in a kayak."

She giggled. "So that's what women are to you! Crab cakes and cup cakes. Ai yai yai! How soon will you have me back?"

"I'm coming into some big money any day now. If it should arrive within the next two hours, getting you back may involve a detour to Tahiti or Cancun or Fiji, maybe all three."

"All right. But I can't clear my calendar for more than a year."

They rode in silence for half an hour and then, after passing a "For Sale" sign, turned onto a dirt road that led up a mountainside. Beryl prepared herself for another climb to the top, but instead the motorcycle soon turned onto a narrower road. Suddenly a steel, slate, and glass A-frame house came into view. The last rays of the setting sun glowed on its triangular face. "It's beautiful!" Beryl exclaimed.

"I thought you'd like it since it could be described as *faux faux alpine*." He took her hand to help her off the cycle. "*Che gelida manina!* You're freezing. I'm so sorry. It never occurred to me that you weren't dressed for this cold wind. Come on. Let's get a fire going."

As they entered the house, Dwight Ingram pointed out various features. "I intended to give you a long, detailed explanation of all my great ideas. But you're cold. The floor is slate. The roof is slate. The glass is double pane. The wood is walnut. The furniture is Eames with one original Shaker piece that belongs in a museum." He knelt in front of the fireplace and lit the kindling that was already laid. He put larger sticks on the fire and finally a few split logs. "Would you like something to drink? The electricity is on. I have both ice and heat. Choose one."

"Is that one of those 'devil or the deep blue sea' things?" she laughed. "Tea. Hot tea, if you have it."

Dwight put the kettle on. On a large round tray he had arranged cookies to form an artful happy face. "I picked these out myself," he said. "The eyebrows are biscotti, the eyes are - now pay attention! - Pfeffernüsse. I'm going to spell that for you. P-f-e-f-f-e-r-n-u-s-s-e. There's an umlaut in there someplace. The mouth is a long crescent, a Japanese Green Tea Cookie. This tray demonstrates why I am so utterly irresistible."

"It amazes me that after years of such charm, a witch somewhere has not turned you into a toad."

"You are bewitched. If you were not, you would see that the creature who is holding this tray is, in fact, a rather large toad. So tell me why you became a private investigator."

The kettle began to whistle. Ingram placed the tray in Beryl's lap and went to make the tea.

"Since you're coming into so much money, why don't you buy this house?"

"Good question. A few days before Catherine died, the folks who owned the place signed a listing agreement with a real estate agent. It's good for ninety days. But if someone meets the price they're asking, the law says that, everything being equal, they have the right to purchase the property. If it were half the price, I couldn't afford it now."

"Why don't you have one of your friends buy it and then sell it back to you once you come into your 'big money'? I take it that the big money is the insurance payout on Catherine's life."

"It is. But I don't have those kinds of friends. In fact, I don't have any friends. That's the price a person pays for having a close relationship with Catherine. She puts an indelible mark on anybody who gets within her reach. You may not know that now, but if you continue to investigate her death, you'll discover it."

"I think I know it now."

"Tell me what you think about Chloe's situation."

"I think she is - let me use a cold climate expression - skating on thin ice."

Ingram closed his eyes. His expression indicated that he had just heard what he most feared hearing. "I love my daughter. I'm scared. What can I do to help her?"

"Things are moving. Recently, at the Philadelphia marina, Sensei watched the chandlers load the Shivadas. My concern is that the yacht is getting ready to leave."

"Why is Chloe on thin ice?"

"Because her mother had some very dangerous associates. Bill may not look dangerous, but he is. People think that she was his 'beard,' but I think he was hers. I think that for so long as she had Handsome Bill on her arm acting like a devoted husband, people figured she had everything a middle-aged woman could want." Beryl stood up and walked to the room's glass face.

Ingram's voice registered bewilderment. "Chloe thinks Bill killed Catherine? What could have happened in the marriage that would make her suspect a rift of that magnitude? Murder? She thinks he murdered her mother?"

"*Does* she?"

The words hung in the air. Ingram stared at the space in front of Beryl. The setting sun's light passed through a nearby tree and struck the glass, casting flickering leaf shadows into the room. It seemed to him as if her breath had frozen into syllables that bobbed in the air in front of her.

Beryl turned and looked at him. His expression of bewilderment had changed into terror. The color drained from his face. He said nothing, but she knew what he was thinking. "Let's not get into possibilities," she said.

"I feel sick," he announced and began to stand up.

Beryl opened the glass door. "Come outside."

A grove of maple trees stood at the side of the house. Beryl followed Ingram as he went to the trees and reached up to hold onto a branch. "I've ruined that kid's life. I'm responsible for all the misery she's known, and there has been so much of it."

"Listen to me," Beryl said. "It's not her misery or her actions, past or present, that concern me now. I think she's in danger. The kind of friends Catherine had are, by their very nature, suspects in her death. Chloe knows things she is not supposed to know. They may not want to leave her in possession of such knowledge.

"We have only a few things to clear up and then we'll retreat to Philadelphia. You'll get your money, and the kids will get theirs. You can buy this house and the houses on the hill, too. My advice is that if people from Sicily or India indicate that they want the properties, do not resist. I don't know how Marietta Post or Wes figure into this - if at all - but the herbal business administrators may have other reasons beside Catherine to maintain contact with Ingram House, Shira Lodge, or Little Flower Haven. If they want to maintain a presence here, do the smart thing. Take your family and move. Buy some land near *Falling Water.*"

They went back into the house. Beryl sat down and began to sip her tea which, she found, was now the perfect temperature. Dwight Ingram picked up the smiling Green Tea crescent cookie and turned it upside down.

They finished their tea without saying another word. As Beryl stood up to leave, she called, "Dwight?"

He was kneeling on the floor, extinguishing the fire. He turned and looked up hopefully at her. "Yes?"

"Put the cookies away in a well-sealed canister. If not, they'll attract bugs."

Ingram stood and picked up the tray. "You could have proposed."

Sensei took a double room and George moved his things into it, giving Beryl the luxury of having a room to herself. She did not enjoy it for long. At 7:30 p.m. George had heard her return from the motorcycle ride. At 7:45 p.m. he knocked on her door. Thinking that perhaps Dwight had forgotten something, she opened the door wide to find George and Sensei standing there. "Good," said George, "You're decent. We need to talk about the case."

They sat on the inside aisle of the beds, Sensei on one side, George and Beryl on the other.

"Now," said Sensei, "I caused you both some embarrassment back there at the restaurant and I don't want to do that again. Lay out this case for me. Who do we have for the murder?"

"Nobody yet," George admitted. "I'm glad you found out that the Little Flower's Haven isn't a 'babies for sale' racket or even a Church property, but we still can't cross Sister Hitler off the suspect list. Catherine was probably not the only source of support for that strange institution."

"I've been thinking about her guests at the Haven," Sensei said. "If a ship anchored off the coast, people could come ashore and into that Haven without anybody knowing it. If there were fugitives or people just needing to be stashed somewhere for safety reasons... or locked up... that would be the perfect place to put them. 'The Little Flower Hideout.' For Catherine to sink so much money into the place, I'm guessing that it had a criminal function. It seems like a stretch - at least to me - to suppose that anyone associated with the place would want to kill Catherine."

Beryl agreed. "I think someone 'up close and personal' killed her."

George explained, "Beryl suspects Chloe. But we lack evidence. Chloe would have needed a confederate or two. Her brother's phone contact with her is too convenient. Danny Brancati is also a possibility. I think that Chloe wanted to see her family reunited; and as long as Catherine was in the picture, that would never happen. And Chloe wanted to see the family reunited specifically in Ingram House. That house is more than a dwelling to them. It doesn't mean anything sentimental to the business associates. Bill may even intend to sell the houses. I don't see him wanting to stay here. Which may be a motive for Chloe to try to pin the crime on Bill. That would get him out of the ownership controversy."

"Wes is Bill's real other half," Beryl added. "Look at the future from Wes's point of view. Skiing isn't an old man's sport. By now his kids are growing up. Life in the islands somewhere may appeal to the two of them. They've been together a long time. And as long as they stay out of sight, the Shivadas administrators may give Bill financial support. If we only knew what they intended. These schemes have a way of playing themselves out. They need to be re-invented... new name... new administrators."

"Pavano might have wanted Catherine dead for a reason we don't know about, but why," George asked, "do it at his birthday party when his mobbed-up friends and relatives were present? You know that they wouldn't appreciate the notoriety. And why was Wes there? Maybe Pavano called him to tell him the news. But knowing how Bill's relatives felt about homosexuality and how the Prince felt about him, Wes was crazy to show up."

"He may have intended for Bill to come down," Beryl noted. "There's still so much we don't know and our own client lies to us."

Sensei had an idea. "Chloe says she found the fake Viagra back in the two houses. She was there before the party. Who knows what was left behind after the party when there had been guests in the house? How about this. You've got a tarp in the back of the pickup. Tomorrow morning I'll hide under the tarp. As you two wait for Morgan to bring Chloe out, I'll get out of the truck and go into the houses. I have my set of lock picks with me. I'll see what I can find. When you're having breakfast with Chloe, George can tell her he wants to look around the two houses when they're finished eating. George can ask her to show him where she found the Viagra. Beryl and Morgan can go into the main house and question Danvers and Pavano about the party and look around. Snoop. I'll get back under the tarp and wait. How does this sound?"

"It sounds good to me," Beryl said. "There's a killer on the loose." She pointed to the Japanese knife she kept in her suitcase. "Bring a weapon."

Sensei grinned. "I didn't bring my knife. If you're babysitting Chloe, you won't need it. Any objections to my borrowing it?"

"None. But... do you know how to use that thing?" Beryl teased.

Sensei stood up and playfully bopped her. "I'll learn by doing."

# FRIDAY, OCTOBER 28, 2011

With Beryl driving, Sensei lying under the tarp, and George sitting in the back seat ready to receive Chloe's sleeping body, the pickup climbed the switchback road and passed Ingram House. When it was safely out of view, Beryl parked.

To divert attention away from Sensei's exit, she got out and walked to the far side of the hilltop.

The morning fog still shrouded the town and lake. It moved, ghost-like, to mix seamlessly with low lying clouds. Here and there the morning sun streaked through and glinted off the tops of a few church spires and tall buildings. The whooshing sound of flapping wings caught her attention and she saw that nearby, from a tall pine, a great blue heron had launched itself, its neck outstretched, its wings raking the air. Beryl watched it gain flight and then, with wings motionless and neck retracted into a pharaonic crown's cobra, it began to glide majestically over the lake before it dipped into the mist, invisibly to skim the water's surface. "Wow," she said aloud. Seeing such a landscape, she thought, was a glorious way to begin a day. She heard footsteps and hurried back to the pickup. Chloe was fully awake.

Morgan got in first and joined George in the rear seat. They drove down the long sloping road. George spoke to Chloe, "Do you have the keys to those two houses? I'd like you to take me back there and show me what's inside."

Morgan Ingram abruptly asked, "Of what possible value is that?"

Beryl answered. "Dr. Ingram, please! The question and answer is between agent and client. You are neither agent nor client. I'll explain the possible value to you when we're alone. But when you question George's motives in doing the job he's been hired to do, you're interfering."

Chloe sighed. "Morg, I haven't been declared insane, not yet, anyway."

Morgan was undeterred. He turned to George, "It's a reasonable question. I'm part owner of those properties. What do you hope to learn?"

Beryl cut off the discussion. "We're 'private investigators' not speakers at a chatuaugua. Personally, I'm beginning to feel like we're conducting an investigation at a town hall or a group therapy session. I'll talk to George; and any question he wants to discuss in public, he'll ask our client about. We've got only one client: Chloe Ingram. All possible relatives, friends, business associates and classmates are not our clients."

George spoke gently. "It's my fault. I shouldn't have brought up visiting the houses until she and I were alone. I'll talk to Chloe before we sit down to have breakfast."

The atmosphere in the pickup truck was tense all the way to the restaurant. As soon as they parked, George and Chloe went off to the side. "I didn't mean to put you on the spot," George said.

"Actually, I don't mind discussing the situation with Morgan - and my father, too." She smiled, "I'm inclined these days to be groggy, and it's good to have a backup memory, so to speak."

Beryl left Morgan to stand alone near the diner's entrance. She signaled Chloe that she had a question for her. "Let's change the subject," she said. "Chloe, you've been on the Shivadas, do you recall what kind of lifeboats they have on board?"

"They have two," Chloe said, "or maybe two and a half. But they're not the ordinary kind. They have one that's like a big rowboat with a motor. Somebody told me the entire crew of twelve plus four guests could sit inside it. They would be exposed to the elements and squeezed together. But there are oars... maybe six of them. If they ran out of gas they'd be able to row. There's a small rowboat they keep inside it - I guess they could use it as shade if they had to. The other boat is a sailboat although it does have a small engine along with a mast and sail that you can raise. I know that they have five-gallon plastic pots of soil that they keep in the rowboat. They raise fresh tomatoes and green peppers and some other vegetables that the Italian chef wants fresh."

"What do they keep in the other boat - the one with the sail?"

Chloe began to laugh. "They have chicken coops in there. They use the poop to fertilize the tomatoes. I hate to tell you this, but for a luxury yacht, they follow some oddly primitive practices. I remember wondering if a cow would be next."

"But I bet the food is good," George said.

"You could forgive any primitive practice after you ate a breakfast of fresh scrambled eggs and peppers with focaccia bread - the kind that's spread with a fresh tomato sauce and cheese. Delicious! You could get fat on that ship, believe me."

George pretended to grouse. "You tell us *that* as I park outside a diner? That comes under 'cruel and unusual' punishment."

Everyone went into the restaurant. Dwight Ingram was waiting in the diner for them to arrive. "Daddy!" Chloe shouted and ran to him. "Oh, Daddy. Nobody told me! And it isn't even my birthday!" He hugged her. They sat in a large booth.

"Before we start talking about the case, why don't we have breakfast," Beryl said. "But there's just one thing... objections and opinions are off limits. The moment anything George and I say something that brings a negative response, I'm cutting the discussion off."

Everyone agreed - at least before the discussion began.

"So," Morgan repeated, as he stirred his 'after breakfast' coffee, "why do you want to look around the two back houses?"

Beryl fielded the question. "Maybe Pavano's associates who were staying in the house left behind something that will help us to discover who imitated Chloe's voice or somehow lured your mother out in Danvers' car. Maybe evidence of something that was used to cause her accident is in there. We need to act expeditiously... before the houses are cleaned thoroughly for the holidays or someone gets a chance to remove something."

Without waiting for Morgan to respond, Beryl asked Chloe, "Tell me, now that you're awake and alert, what do you think was Pavano's motive for killing your mother?"

"I know why. I was hoping you'd find evidence on your own so that I could stay out of this. I'm already too involved."

Beryl was emphatic. "If you know why he killed your mother, then tell us. There's been enough subterfuge and manipulation and deception. Just tell us."

Chloe sighed. "You know how afraid Bill was that his Sicilian friends would find out about Wes. They're ruthless and hateful. They would kill him and Wes."

"Yes, Honey," Ingram said, "but why would that make him want to kill your mother? And those guys weren't born yesterday. They've had to have known the score about Bill and Wes."

"There's some family history that I've kept to myself for a long time, and I guess it's time for me to tell." She paused for a final moment to reconsider. Then she took a deep breath. "After I had the abortion, Danny would not speak to me. He joined the Army, and life in this town became unbearable. At school, I could barely concentrate. I agreed to spend time with my mother on the yacht.

"We were in Morocco. It was a nice day. My mother was talking to business people and I was bored stiff. I went ashore and walked through the bazaar. I saw Bill go into a tented stall that sold women's sexy 'harem girl' dancing outfits. I went into the tent and heard him talking. Nobody was out front at the counter, so I peeked around a drape. Bill was posing in front of a mirror wearing a harem girl's veil. I had no idea he was gay. That's how naive I was.

"Back at the ship, I searched his personal stuff and found a vial of stilbestrol in his medicine chest. It's one of those estrogen hormones they give steers to make them think they're cows and grow fat. Then I found his cache of women's clothes and shoes. I hated him so much because of the abortion that I wanted to get pictures of him in those clothes. Bill is not 'computer savvy.' Every day I'd leave my laptop on with the video camera running. For two days, I got nothing. On the third day he danced on camera, in full costume.

"I couldn't believe what was on the video. His nipples were pierced with rings. Then he put the costume's semi-bra on. He wore clip-on dangling earrings, but the funniest thing was a new tattoo he had just gotten. On the skin where his pubic hair would be, a tattoo artist had recently written 'Wes.' The area had been shaved. I guess he expected that when the hair grew back it would cover the tattoo. Everything came together. I used to wonder why my mother dragged me up to Shira Lodge to get skiing lessons. I guess it was to give a 'family' cover to Bill's visit."

Chloe paused and looked around, embarrassed to have everyone's eyes on her. "I'm not the best raconteur around, so please don't be angry with me if I'm not clear or articulate. It hasn't been easy for me to figure things out."

Dwight Ingram smiled, "Chloe, when I think of what you've been through and how you sit here now, lookin' like a cover girl… I'm so proud of you. Keep talkin', girl. You're doin' fine. Besides, this is one helluva story!"

Chloe smiled. "Just wait. It gets better. My mother and Bill had a deal. When my Aunt Marietta took over Little Flower's Haven, the place needed repairs and the nuns were practically starving. It became my mother's 'Holy Task' to save the nuns and the building. Her herbal medicine business and the charities were becoming very profitable, so she sank a lot of money into the project.

"At the time, Shira Lodge was also in financial trouble and Bill wanted to help. So she agreed that for as long as Wes and Bill maintained a respectable façade, Bill could give as much money to Wes as she gave to her sister. Every month Marietta got a check and Wes got a bag of cash.

"Let me back up a bit. When my mother first met Bill, he had a yoga studio and an ayurvedic health products business. When she married him they teamed up to form a new business which really started to expand.

"Bill originally had a guy in China who produced the herbal products. But then, when the company's star began to rise, they were noticed by a group of Sicilian entrepreneurs who bought into the business. The Chinese guy started to get greedy, and they replaced him with a supplier from India.

"The top Sicilian guy was named Cardinale. They called him 'The Prince.' He idolized my mother. He now weighs a ton, but then he was well built and handsome. He was," she turned to Ingram, "more 'beef cake' than you, Dad."

"Impossible!" Ingram quipped.

"Cardinale thought my mom was a madonna. He commissioned half a dozen paintings of her as the Virgin Mary. One of them is hanging in the entry of the Little Flower's Haven.

"Bill and Wes would go away together for the months of September and April. Bill would start those stilbestrol hormone injections in the month before he went and stop them before he came home. But during those months he actually dressed like a woman. They would go off to exotic places. My mother and some real nuns would visit refugee camps. The Shivadas' herbal supply company got many contracts.

"I had that video of Bill in my possession for several years. I never intended to use it. You know how it is. Danny was married. Sharp edges get dull. I'm not the revengeful type. But then in Spain this summer, my mother got sick. She had ovarian cysts. Her doctor put her in a very strict Catholic hospital. They had a policy of not removing a woman's sexual organs without the husband's 'consent and approval.' Incidentally, there are several major religious groups that do that. Bill and Wes Richter were staying at a hotel in Majorca at the time. The hospital admissions clerk asked my mother where her husband was, and, thinking that they needed it for emergency use, she told the clerk the name of the hotel. When it was decided that my mom needed to have surgery, they contacted a priest in that Majorca resort town and asked him go to the hotel and get Bill's consent for the procedure. Because of passport regulations, Bill had to register under his own name. Then he'd transform into this mysterious lady who had an adjoining room with Wes. The confused priest went to Bill's room and found the 'Lady Bill,' but he didn't know it. He asked

Bill where Bill was and Bill said he didn't know." Everyone at the table laughed merrily.

"The story was hilarious and it got back to Sicily. My mother was humiliated. She would write to Cardinale in English and he'd use the automatic translation service on the net. It's a clunky translation, but it allowed them to communicate both ways. Bill might not have been able to access the communications, but I had no problem. I could access her computer in Hawaii. She only used it to talk to the big guy. Cardinale said he'd handle it and advised her to insist it was a lie - after all, there were no photos of the Lady Bill. She should also show her support for Bill by giving him a big birthday party on October 1st. She sent out invitations.

"While she and Bill were back on the yacht, I was in Hawaii doing research on volcanic gases. Morgan called me to gab - we constantly talk. He told me that he had heard Danny was very unhappy in his marriage, and that his wife had left him. He still worked at the gas station. So I called him. We both cried on the phone. He asked me to come home and I did. Then my mother and Bill returned. Danvers had seen Danny and me together in one of the two houses and told Bill. He and my mother went crazy screaming at me. Then Bill said something insulting about the way my mother raised me - that I would let a low life bum sneak into his house. My mother asked him how he dared to criticize anyone else... when Wes came whenever he pleased. They didn't let up. Bill didn't know that he and Wes had been 'exposed' in Majorca and that my mother was shielding him from trouble with the Sicilian folks. He called me a tramp and threatened to call Danny at the gas station. He even threatened to call Dan's wife in Germany. That did it! This time I wasn't taking it. I knew that my mom thought there was no photographic proof of Bill's sexuality, so I showed her the video of Bill the Belly Dancer. She knew that I had kept the video secret for years. She could tell by the furniture in the room how old the video was. I think it made her realize how unreasonable she had been. We talked rationally, for a change.

"I told her I had kept it because I was afraid of what Bill and Wes might do to her. She had re-written her will. If she died, he'd get half of her estate even with the restrictions she had written into it. If anyone could prove the story about Majorca, she'd look like a fool or a freak... an object of pity or derision. There she was lying in a hospital bed while her husband was running around wearing a sundress and lipstick. My mother would never permit herself to be described as either a fool or a freak. And Cardinale would never let that happen.

"It was Friday, September 30th, and the guests were beginning to arrive in town for the big party. She asked me to make copies of the video. She told Bill that their deal mandated 'discretion' and he had been far from discreet. He was finished, and if he didn't go gracefully, the copies, which she had cached with various people, would be made public here and in Sicily and Florence. I never figured he would react until he got all the copies back. I was wrong."

Morgan Ingram rubbed his face. "Finally, we find his motive! But why didn't you ever tell me what was going on? And Daddy, too? We were so sick with worry about you. Why would you put us through all this? And you let them give you powerful tranquilizers! They could have put cyanide in those capsules!"

George returned to the murderous act. "How do you think Bill pulled it off?" he asked Chloe.

"Good Lord, Mr. Wagner!" Chloe exclaimed. "That's why we hired you! I don't know. My dad says that Wes was around the house that night. Maybe he knows."

"How far is *Shira Lodge* from here?" George asked.

"An hour or so's drive," Chloe estimated.

"We really ought to interview Wes," Beryl said. "I had thought we could avoid it, but now that we know he was at the scene at the time of the crime, we should talk to him."

"Morgan really doesn't know the way," Chloe said. "I do. So why don't we girls stay together and the guys– but not Daddy! I don't want to get him involved any more than he is – can go up to the houses and see if they can uncover or learn anything that will help solve the mystery."

Dwight Ingram objected. "What do you mean, 'but not Daddy'? I can help search, too."

Chloe snarled, "No! Absolutely not! You have to stay out of it!" She looked around. "Bill knows that if he's charged with killing my mother, he won't inherit anything. And if he needs money for a lawyer or a ticket to Brazil, he'd try to get his hands on your insurance payout. He'd have Danvers and his friends to help him. So, no way."

"And you think I'd just hand it over?" Dwight asked.

"You would if someone held a knife to Morg's throat or mine." She turned to Beryl and George. "It suited my mother's vanity to let the world think that there was no love at all between my father and Morgan and me."

"All right, then," Dwight Ingram sighed. "I'll either be at the Y or with Ross D'Angelo, minding my own business."

"There's a car rental place down the street," Beryl noted. "Let's rent a car and drive up to the Lodge right now."

Sensei pulled on surgical gloves and selected the house that was farthest from the main house. He went to the rear door and inserted a tension wrench into the lock. He raked a pick over the pins, wiggling it until all the pins aligned. The door opened easily. He left his shoes on the doorstep and went inside.

The exterior door led directly into the kitchen, and even in this usually well-lit part of any house, the blinds were closed and heavy curtains were drawn over them. From what he could see as he stood and looked towards the interior rooms, the drapes and venetian blinds had all been closed. Only at the edges of the window coverings did any light enter.

He flicked on the light switch, but no lights went on. He spread apart the curtains over the sink and gained enough light to find the garbage disposal's switch. Again, no response. The electricity, he surmised, had been turned off at the outside circuit breaker panel.

Leaving the rear door closed but unlocked, he moved through the dimly lit interior. The kitchen and hallway floors were ceramic tile. He entered a carpeted bedroom and opened the drapes. Immediately he could see that his feet had disturbed the curved pattern of vacuum cleaner ridges that led back to the door he had entered. If he had stepped in wet cement he could not have made a more noticeable impression than he made when he walked across the deep pile of the freshly vacuumed carpet. Sensei knew that to an experienced housekeeper the strokes left by the cleaner would be as recognizable as an artist's brush strokes would be to the artist. He would have to restore the integrity of the pattern as he left the room.

He returned to the kitchen to look for an instrument that could make carpet ridges. He had hoped to find forks, but all the silverware had been removed. Under the sink he found several tall cardboard cans of cleanser. He selected one that was nearly empty, exited onto the back step, and emptied the remaining powder onto the morning breeze. Then he stepped on the cardboard can until it was flat. He took his knife from its scabbard which hung slightly left of center on the inside of his baggy pants, and with the speed and accuracy of a chef, he deftly cut a line of teeth into the edge. He returned to the bedroom and opened the drape far enough to be able to see the room clearly.

Nothing seemed to be out of place. He looked in the standard sliding-door closets and found an assortment of rainwear - raincoats, galoshes, boots. He checked all the pockets and the insides of the footwear and found nothing. The shelf was empty. He opened the dresser drawers and in one he found an opened carton of Viagra boxes. Of the original twelve boxes, four had been removed. Sensei looked under the bed and under the skirts of the two upholstered chairs that flanked a small circular table. Nothing was there. The bedside table's drawer was also empty. The bathroom contained nothing that suggested that a human being had ever used the facility. He closed the drape, leaving just a sliver of light so that he could discern the pattern in the rug's pile.

He dropped to his knees and crawling backwards he made sweeping motions into the rug with the ridging tool as he combed his way out of the rooms.

He moved more carefully into the next bedroom and bathroom, disturbing as little of the pattern in the pile as possible. Again, there was nothing in the room, not even rainwear. The third bedroom also yielded nothing. He covered his tracks as he left the room.

In the den he found a desk, and in the desk he finally found something that interested him: *Shivadas* stationery and the stationery of five other companies located in Italy and India. He removed a sheet from each kind of letterhead, folded the sheet in the standard third-fold, and inserted each into its corresponding envelope. He put the envelopes into his jacket's inside pocket and, seeing that the room yielded nothing else, he passed a heavier door, opened it, and saw that it led into the garage.

Someone had been in the living room. The air was still redolent with the scent of fine tobacco. He lifted a corner of the drape that covered a window and could see that the rug's surface had been much disturbed. There was a cigar butt in an ashtray on a table beside a large Chippendale chair. Suddenly he heard a car pull up outside. Sensei ran to escape through the kitchen door when he heard someone shout, "The circuit breaker switch has to be thrown." Sensei quickly closed the kitchen curtains just as he heard someone opening the circuit breaker panel. He immediately realized that he could not exit the way he had entered. He ran back into the living room and hid behind a large upholstered chair in the corner of the room just as distorted human shapes appeared in the front door's leaded glass panel. Sensei stayed crouched behind the chair. A key had been inserted into the front door's lock.

A woman entered the living room and said, "I'll see if the lamp works." She came to the lamp nearest Sensei's hiding place and pulled a chain. The room was illuminated. "Ok," she shouted, "the juice is on."

A man's voice said, "Anybody been in here? Check it!" The man gave an order in Italian and in another moment several lamps were lit. Now the woman walked back towards the kitchen. She stopped in the doorway of each bedroom and flicked on the light switch. "All clear," she finally called. "Nobody's been here."

Sensei began a silent prayer of thanksgiving for having remembered to restore the patterns in the rug; and then he heard a car pull up, doors slam shut, footsteps walk to the house, and voices speaking in Italian. An apparently large dog growled, barked, and strained at its collar. Released, it made a direct attack on the man behind the chair. Its jaw clamped down on Sensei's foot and instinctively, Sensei, with one fierce chopping motion, struck the dog across its eyes, blinding the animal. The dog released his foot and yelped in pain. Sensei looked up to see two Glock semi-automatics pointed at him. In Italian, he was ordered, he assumed, to get up.

"Who the hell are you?" Bill Pavano asked.

Sensei tried to fake a Chinese accent. "I nobody. I look for loot, for stuff I hock, stuff pawnshop buy. I find nothing. I hear you come. I hide."

"Danvers! Come here!" Pavano called. Sensei had his back to the hallway but he heard her walk towards the living room. "You know this guy?"

"Turn around!" he ordered. Sensei turned around.

"No," she said. "I don't know him. I've never seen him before."

The dog was still yelping in pain. A man cursed in Italian. Pavano looked at Sensei. "If you hurt His Grace's dog, you will pay."

"I pay. I pay. I no have much money. What I have I give him. He give to vet for dog."

"No, Chinaman. You pay with life." Pavano snarled. "Danvers! Pat him down."

The woman slapped his arms, armpits, chest, and back and down the outside of his hips, thighs, and lower legs. She did not check the inside of his thighs and therefore did not discover the knife. "He's not armed," she said. Sensei, who had a secret fear that he would one day be decapitated with his own blade, relaxed.

The room was suddenly filled with people. Pavano, Danvers, Sensei, three rough characters who seemed to be bodyguards, and a dog that continued to howl in pain. Now in the doorway stood an extremely fat man. Pavano deferentially addressed him, "*Grace, prego si sieda, per favore.*"

The fat man waddled across the living room and dropped into the Chippendale chair. "*Perché il mio cane soffre?*"

"What did you do to His Grace's dog?" demanded Pavano.

"He bite my foot." Blood was filling Sensei's white sock. "I make him let go my foot."

"That's what he did to you, you idiot! What did you do to him to cause him so much pain?"

The fat man began to blubber as he tried to comfort the dog. *"Il mio cane! Cieco! Per sempre? Il mio vecchio cane. Il mio amico."*

"I think," said Pavano in a hissing voice, "that we will cut you up and feed you to him. His Grace wants to know if he is permanently blind."

"I think he is," Sensei said.

Pavano infused his voice with tears. *"Grace... Il tuo cane rimarrá cieco per sempre."*

The fat man said something in Italian to one of the men who dragged the howling animal outside and shot it.

Of all the sounds that Sensei expected to hear next, the last one was the engine of George's pickup. Morgan Ingram's voice was next. "What's happening here?" he called. "Did you just shoot that dog?" The man who shot the dog did not answer. Instead, Bill Pavano walked to the doorway and invited George and Morgan to come into the house.

A half hour after they left the breakfast diner, Beryl and Chloe were taking a series of two-lane blacktops into the southern Green Mountains of Vermont. The maple leaves had turned golden and red but had not yet become sere. When they blew off the trees they made swinging arcs in the air, back and forth, as they rocked their way down to earth. A cold air mass from Canada had hastened the leaves' departure from the trees and created a riot of color on the road. They drove in silence, made speechless by the beauty.

As they ascended the mountain on which the lodge was located, they were passed by a police car that had its emergency lights on. Beryl saw the red and blue flashes in her rear view mirror and supposed, for a moment, that she had exceeded the speed limit. When the car passed her, she said, "That's a relief! I thought it was gonna be trouble."

"Maybe it is trouble," Chloe said. "The road ends at the lodge."

Two other police cars and an emergency rescue vehicle passed before they got to the lodge's parking lot. The ambulance, its rear doors open, was parked at the entrance. Two white uniformed attendants sat off to the side, smoking cigarettes. "The person they came for is dead," Beryl said. "Those guys are in no hurry to receive the victim of what has obviously been a crime, a murder or murders."

"Does that mean the forensic people are allowed to 'do their thing,' like on TV shows?"

"Yes. That's exactly what it means. The corpse stays *in situ* until they're finished. And nobody will be allowed near the crime scene for fear of contaminating it."

"So, we just wait?"

"Yes, until we see some plainclothes cops come out. Then we can approach them and find out what's going on. Until then, it is best to stay out of the way."

Twenty minutes passed and finally two men wearing ordinary clothing came out and stood talking to one of the uniformed police officers. "Let's go see what we can find out," Beryl said as she opened the car door. Chloe followed.

As they approached one of the investigators, a lodge bellhop walked up to him and pointed to Chloe and whispered something.

"Girl, you've been recognized," Beryl said, surprised. "When is the last time you were here? I thought you hadn't seen the place since you were a kid."

"No. I was here with my mother last Christmas." The bellhop continued to point at Chloe and give information to the police investigator.

"He has a good memory."

The police investigator signaled Beryl to stop and talk. She took her business card out of her purse and handed it to him as she flipped her wallet open to display her license.

"You here to see anybody in particular?" he asked, glancing at her credentials.

"We had wanted to speak to the owner, Wes Richter. Please tell me he's not the subject of all this interest."

"I'm afraid he is. Shot. Right in the back of his head."

"Why, Lieutenant, are you suggesting an execution-style murder?"

"Or one that was made to look like one. What's your interest in Richter?"

"I'm working another case, an accidental death, or 'one that was made to look like one.'"

"Whose?"

"Catherine Post Ingram Pavano's death on October 1st, in Lake George."

"Ah, Bill Pavano's wife who drove off a cliff. And this is her daughter, Chloe."

"The same. Any suspects with this case?"

"Not yet, but I'd like you to come down to my office and discuss this connection to the victim. Now, if you don't mind."

"No, unfortunately I do mind. My partner, the Wagner on that card I just gave you, is a retired investigator with the Philadelphia Police. You can check him out. He retired on disability. He's not exactly defenseless, but with a killer on the loose, I'm not going to tell you in person what I can tell you on the phone. He may have just walked into a trap. Here's my cell number." She took back her card and wrote the number on it. "We're at the Lago Motel in Lake George with another operative. Give me your card and I'll keep you in the loop."

The investigator gave Beryl his card. She pushed it down into her purse without looking at it as she took Chloe's arm and rushed back to her rental car.

Bill Pavano stood in the doorway and smirked. "Mr. Wagner and *Doctor* Ingram. Come in and meet some of Catherine's and my old friends. We've just caught a Chinese burglar. Do you happen to know him?"

George and Morgan entered the house and nodded a greeting to the big man who was sitting in the Chippendale chair.

Morgan looked at Sensei. "Is this the burglar?"

"What were you looking for?" George asked.

"Just stuff for pawn shop. I need money for food. No work around."

"Call the cops," George advised. "You caught him red-handed."

"He was hiding behind that chair," Pavano said. "The dog got him."

"And for *that* you killed the dog?" Morgan asked incredulously. "You should have shot the son of a bitch who tried to rob us, not the dog."

"Ah, but my dear stepson, he permanently blinded the dog. His Grace merely put the poor beast out of its misery."

"Oh," George suddenly changed his tone to one of respect. "*Signore*... Cardinale? Please tell His Grace that we apologize. Such an act requires courage and compassion. It is a difficult kindness."

Pavano responded as if he intended to force George into admitting that he possessed secret information. "How did you know His Grace's name?"

Morgan Ingram affected a cavalier expression. "I told him His Grace's name. We saw him get out of the car just as we drove around the curve. Tell His Grace what Mr. Wagner said about a difficult act of kindness, the courage and compassion it requires."

George and Morgan stood quietly as Pavano translated George's remark and explained how George knew his name.

Cardinale asked Pavano to thank George for understanding and to ask him if he had ever killed his own pet dog. George replied that he hadn't killed a dog, but on two occasions he had to put down horses that he loved. It was a lie of course. George had been on a horse only a few times in his life. He was told to mount the horse from the horse's left. Beyond that he knew nothing about horses. He deliberately avoided looking at Sensei.

His Grace issued commands and questions. He sent Danvers down to the main house to bring iced tea to them, along with sprigs of spearmint. Did George and Morgan prefer lemon or spearmint? They preferred whatever His Grace was having. He ordered that Sensei's hands be bound behind his back and that he be put in the garage. Plastic zip ties were tightened on Sensei's wrists, and he was dragged from the room. With a jerk of his head Cardinale indicated that one of the men should guard Sensei.

Cardinale then asked what was wrong with George's hand. When Pavano translated that question, he looked at George and smirked again. "I told you that you should wear a glove."

"Forgive me, Your Grace," George said, trying to remember the attitude of the supplicant in *The Godfather*. "I don't speak your language." (He pointed at his tongue and wagged his finger negatively.) "But I (he pointed at himself) was a policeman. *Policia*." He pointed to his back and turned to show him the approximate area. "Big bullet. It came out the front. Then, conforming his left hand into a pistol, he fired his thumb. "I was shot here." He indicated the through and through shot from back to front of his shoulder. Then he turned and pulled up his pant leg and finger shot his knee, showing him the many scars on his knee.

Cardinale asked to see the scars on his shoulder. George stood up and took off his jacket and shirt and pulled his undershirt over his head. Pavano looked up at him with obvious disdain. Cardinale watched Pavano as Pavano looked at George. "Tell him," he said in Italian, "to make muscles like Mr. Universe."

George laughed and comically tried to mimic the show-off postures of body-builders. Cardinale wore no belt around his waist and perspiration made his loose shirt cling to his skin. When he laughed, he shook like aspic as the rolls of fat undulated down his body. Then George turned and knelt to show his back to the fat man who said, "*Mamma!*" and then asked in Italian how long all those operations took. George answered in what he hoped was a romance language. "*Una año,*" and raised his index finger. Then he opened and closed his fists twice. "Twenty operations. *Mucho dolor.*" It was actually twenty-two operations but the two extra seemed to be bragging.

"*Venti... operazioni,*" His Grace said, shaking his head in sympathy. Then the atmosphere in the room suddenly changed. Cardinale asked Pavano what he thought about George's muscles.

"Frankly, Your Grace," he frowned, "*Alcuni sono brutti... deformi.*" Pavano seemed oblivious to the change in Cardinale's attitude; but both George and Morgan suspected what the change indicated.

"*Dov'è il tuo amico Wes?*" asked His Grace.

George, hearing the name 'Wes,' knew precisely what was coming. He quickly put his shirt on.

Pavano shrugged. "*E' a casa.*"

"*A casa di Dio o del Diavolo?*"

Pavano shrugged his shoulders. "Only God knows," he said, trying to seem indifferent.

"*Chiamatelo,*" said His Grace.

Pavano smiled pleasantly, but a shadow of concern crept across his face. He took out his cellphone and called the Lodge. Someone answered. Pavano asked for Wes and was told not to tie up the line. The police were there. Wes had been shot. Wes was dead. The call was disconnected.

Pavano stood there staring at the phone in his hand. He neither said nor did anything. He did not even breathe. He simply stared quizzically at the phone.

His Grace said, "*Omosessuale.*" It was not said in an accusatory manner, but simply a word said aloud, without emotion.

Pavano suddenly drew in breath with a frantic gasp, as if he had finally emerged from a deep and long underwater entanglement. As soon as he had sucked in all the air his lungs could hold, he began to enunciate a long "A" vowel until one of the men punched him on his ear, and Pavano collapsed silently onto the living room floor.

With his interpreter gone, further attempts at conversation were useless. Danvers was coming with a tray filled with glasses, an ice bucket, and a large pitcher of iced tea and spearmint.

She came into the living room, stepped over Pavano's body, and placed the tray on the coffee table. She held up a blue packet of sugar substitute for His Grace to see. He nodded and she began ritualistically to use tongs to put two ice cubes into an eight-inch tumbler, pour the tea over them and, using the tongs again, to extract a sprig of spearmint from the pitcher and put it on top of the glass as a garnish.

She prepared and, starting with His Grace, distributed the glasses of iced tea. Everyone waited for Cardinale to sip his, and once his approval was given, everyone drank.

Nobody said anything until all of the iced tea had been drunk. And then His Grace directed Morgan and George to return to the main house.

Both thanked him for his graciousness and left.

As they got into the pickup to turn it around and drive the short distance to Ingram House, George said, "If anything happens to Percy, I'm gonna kill that pig myself. Now, how the hell are we gonna get him out?"

"His foot looked like it was bleeding bad," Morgan said. "He needs to get to a hospital."

George grunted. He parked at Ingram House and checked to see that his gun was still in the glove compartment. "I don't see an alternative. Call 9-1-1 and direct them to the third house."

"The emergency vehicle won't drive up the steep road. They'll go all the way around. It'll take half an hour."

"What choice do we have? Call them."

Morgan turned his phone on. "Wait! I've got a text from Chloe. She says Wes was shot dead and they're on their way back."

"How long ago did it come in?"

"Twenty minutes ago. But it doesn't say where they were when Chloe sent it."

George looked back to see one of the cars that had been parked at the third house come around the curve, heading towards the steep road. "Check this car!" he whispered.

Morgan strained to look. "Danvers is in the passenger's seat. One of the thugs is driving. They're probably going out to buy lunch."

George formed a plan. "This is our chance! Do you have a gun?"

"A flare gun?"

George groaned. He looked sideways at Morgan. "*A weapon*! Are there any weapons in the house?" He took his Colt from the glove compartment and walked to the front door. "*Think*! You've gotta' have some weapons in here!"

Morgan tried to be helpful. "No other guns that I know of. I've got a bow and arrows. That's a weapon! I'm considered a crack shot." He qualified his claim. "At least I was when I was in prep school. I haven't shot anything lately."

George repeated to himself, "A bow and arrows?" He checked his clip.

Morgan unlocked the door and stepped inside. "I could bring down a full grown deer. I'll show you." He hurried through the foyer. "I'll be right back."

George went into the domed room and sat down. He tried to refine his plan. Pavano was likely dead or too emotional to be of any use to Cardinale, who was also no threat. There were two guards with two Glocks. With a little luck, Cardinale would suspect that Sensei was not a random burglar - as he pretended to be, and he'd keep one of the guards stationed in the garage. The other guard would be in the living room with Cardinale. In this case, the element of surprise was the equivalent of a second gun. If the two guards were together, George would not have a chance unless Morgan drew one guard's attention. He envisioned a large compound bow which, he thought, with all its wheels and pulleys would have a threatening look to it. All he needed was a moment's distraction.

Morgan returned, carrying a quiver and a long unstrung fiberglass "recurved" bow. "Here," he said weakly, placing them on the seat beside George.

George took a deep breath. The threat had vanished. "What does that do? Poke 'em to death? That thing won't scare anybody. We'll enter through the kitchen. Sensei was in his stocking feet, so no doubt he left his shoes outside. Since they weren't at the front door, they must be at the kitchen door."

"And...?" Morgan did not grasp the significance.

"And that means he intended to leave by the kitchen door and wouldn't have re-locked it!"

"Oh. The back door may be unlocked for us."

"With Danvers and one of the bodyguards gone, that leaves only Cardinale and two guards."

"Pavano will be there."

"Pavano is not likely to be a threat to anyone!" George was running out of patience. "There is just you and your bow and arrows and me and my Colt against two thugs with Glocks!"

"About my bow and arrows," Morgan said, "I can't find my bowstring." He picked up the bow. "Without that string, I can't shoot an arrow."

"Great," said George, feeling both anger and frustration. He flicked his finger through an arrow's fletching. "Are you gonna tickle 'em to death?" He pulled a couple of arrows out of the quiver. "How are you at darts? Maybe you could throw them at the guy with the Glock. Aim for the little hole."

"Look!" Morgan yelled, pointing at the quiver. "The bowstring's in there! You found it when you pulled out the arrows." He quickly nocked the string onto one end of the bow, then bent the bow backwards, bracing it with his leg. "There!" he said, completing the stringing. "It's a weapon now! We can sneak up to the back door! Which room do you want? The living room or the garage?" He fumbled with an arrow as he tried to nock it.

George groaned. He stood up and watched as the arrow, feathers down, bounced on the slate floor. "Don't shoot yourself!"

Morgan tried to reposition the arrow. "The string is a little too thin for the nock," he explained. "It should fit snug. You have to be careful handling these arrows. They're for hunting."

George began to stride across the room. "Let's get moving!" He paused at the door and looked back to see Morgan trying to put his right arm and shoulder through the quiver's sling. "Jesus!" he hissed. "Look at us. Me with a weak trigger-finger and you with that goddamned toy!"

They circled around to the back of the houses and approached the last house from the rear.

Sensei's shoes were on the kitchen doorstep. George drew his gun, checked the safety and slide, making sure it was ready to fire. Then he turned the knob, pushed the door open, and went inside. Morgan followed.

As they turned into the hallway, they could hear Pavano calling out Wes's name and sobbing uncontrollably. Morgan touched George's arm and pointed at a door. He mouthed the word, "Garage."

George nodded. "At the count of five," he whispered, "we go. You," he pointed at the garage door. Morgan nodded. George began the count. "One, two, three, four, five."

With Morgan leading, they proceeded down the hall. The door to the garage opened into the hallway. Without waiting for George to pass, Morgan turned the knob and pulled the door open, blocking George who in disgust pushed the door closed again as he bounded towards the living room.

Cardinale's bodyguard turned and reached into his shoulder holster to draw his gun. George shot first and the man fell forward onto the floor. Pavano, shrieking like a child, made two fists of his hands which he shook in front of him as though they were maracas.

When Morgan tried to enter the garage he mistakenly held his bow horizontally and the bow got caught in the doorway. The garage was an unexpected step down, and as he tried to correct his position, he stumbled and fell. A bullet passed his head within inches, and the arrow skidded on the floor like an old coat hanger. He looked up helplessly to see the guard laugh at him and press his gun's muzzle against Sensei's ear.

*"J'adoube,"* said Sensei, using the chess term to refer both to the misused arrow and to the gun pointed into his ear. The guard shouted something in Italian.

Morgan shouted, "He's got Sensei in here, and me!"

Pavano stopped shaking and shrieking. He watched George and jeered at him, "You lose! You lose!"

George looked at Cardinale and shrugged. The big man nodded in sympathy. George put his gun on the coffee table and called, "You ok, Perce?"

Sensei answered, "I'm fine. Come and join the party."

George went to the garage doorway and surveyed the disaster. He did not notice that Pavano had followed him. The guard was still laughing at Morgan and even George had to smile. "What the hell was I thinking?" he asked the guard who understood perfectly what he meant.

Suddenly, Pavano shoved George hard, propelling him down onto the concrete floor. George, landing on his damaged knee, stifled a long howl of pain as he grabbed his knee and grimaced. Pavano jumped down into the garage and began to kick George. With manic glee he yelled a triumphant cry with each kick. The guard held up two zip ties and ordered Pavano to put the ties on the two prisoners. Pavano snatched the ties. Morgan held his hands behind him and Pavano slipped the loops over his wrists. He tightened the loops and kicked Morgan several times before he turned to George who obediently held his hands behind him. Giggling hysterically, Pavano secured the tie. "Get over there beside the Chinese burglar. Keystone Cops! You're a bunch of Keystone Cops."

On their knees, George and Morgan crept to either side of Sensei.

Pavano picked up the bow and began plucking the string as though it were a lyre. "How amusing!" he said. "I'll play this for Wes!" He carried it into the living room to show Cardinale.

George looked at the guard. *"Loco. Luna loco."* The guard nodded. Then George turned to Morgan. "Bill is nuts with grief. He's lost his marbles." Then he looked at the quiver. "So have I. What the hell was I thinking?"

A car pulled up and parked near the front door. They could hear Danvers' voice. George and Morgan looked at each other, surprised that she had returned so quickly.

She came into the garage and placed a shopping bag on top of a worktable that stood beside the laundry sink. A few ears of ornamental 'Indian' corn lay on top of the items in the bag. Each cob of multi-colored kernels was topped with its dried husk pulled back. They were intended to be hung on doors or laid in display bowls. George and Sensei exchanged a look of dread. Pavano, his grief converted now into demented ravings, had no clue whatsoever of the intended purpose of the cobs. He sashayed around the garage in a bizarre victory dance.

The guard who had gone with Danvers came into the garage and, in one swift movement, clutched Pavano's hair and dragged him into the hallway. Pavano screamed.

Sensei looked at George and Morgan. "It's best to remember the refugees," he said. A bathroom door slammed. Pavano screamed continually.

After fifteen minutes of listening to the torture, the guard in the garage shouted something in Italian and laughed. Cardinale answered. The bathroom door opened. The screams subsided into sobs. The guard who had been with Pavano changed places with the guard in the garage. During the change, Morgan drew a hunting arrow out of the quiver and pushed it toward Sensei's hands. While the guard went to the laundry sink to wash Pavano's blood from his hands, Morgan pulled a second arrow out of the quiver for his own use.

Again the screaming began. Danvers came into the garage and got a mop, bucket, cleaning liquid, and a roll of paper towels. She said nothing, and no one tried to speak to her.

Cardinale got up from his chair, picked up the dead bodyguard's Glock, and waddled down the hall to the bathroom. He stood in the doorway and spoke in a threatening tone to Pavano, who pleaded and wept. Cardinale then began to shout, *"Hanno disonorato la mia Caterina!"*

George, Sensei, and Morgan understood the meaning, but in the event that they had failed to grasp it, the guard explained, "He dishonor the *signora*." As soon as Cardinale finished his condemnations, the screaming resumed.

The guard in the garage began to sing *Santa Lucia* at the top of his voice. As they listened, Sensei nudged George and bent forward to let him see that his hands were free. He had sliced through the plastic tie with the strong, razor-sharp arrowhead. Morgan, too, had sliced through his restraints. George raised his eyebrows, indicating his surprise to learn that the arrows were, in fact, weapons of considerable power. It frustrated and saddened him to realize that he lacked the dexterity to cut his own tie. And then he looked up to see the door push open a bit and the muzzle of Beryl's Beretta peek around the doorjamb.

Sensei saw the muzzle too. He and George looked at each other and then at Morgan. There was a problem. Morgan sat on the floor closest to Beryl, Sensei was next, and third was George. The man Beryl needed to hit was the fourth man. George immediately coughed and bent his head as far forward as he could. Sensei did the same, but Morgan did not understand that he was in the line of fire and continued to sit up, shielding the target.

Sensei put his arm around Morgan's shoulder and showed five open fingers to Beryl. He began to close them, while simultaneously nudging George: one, two, three, four, and on the count of five he pushed Morgan's torso down and George bent over as Beryl fired. The guard had turned to look at Sensei and the bullet pierced his eye.

Immediately, Cardinale turned around, took a step into the hall, and pointed his gun at Beryl. He fired once, and missed. The bathroom door was on the same side of the corridor as the garage door. Beryl stepped as far to her right as she could and fired the Beretta twice, one shot entered Cardinale's chest and the other scraped his forehead, severing an artery. Blood squirted into the air and he collapsed in a heap where he had stood. Suddenly a mop handle came down across Beryl's arm as Danvers screamed a kind of war cry. Beryl's gun slid across the hallway. Chloe pushed Beryl aside and dove for the gun, grabbing it a moment before Danvers's outstretched fingers touched it. Chloe turned the gun into Danvers's chest and fired it. The housekeeper gasped with gurgling, rasping breaths, and then she grew limp and fell forward, face-down on the floor.

Cardinale's spurting arterial blood drenched everything in the bathroom. The guard who had been torturing Pavano drew his gun and pointed it while trying to wipe the blood from his eyes. It was useless: the stream of blood pulsed steadily at him. He could not change his position because the fat man's body blocked the entrance. He grabbed Pavano and tried to use him as a shield against the streaming blood. Pavano shrieked hysterically and struggled to wrench himself free. The guard fired wildly into the hall, but Chloe, ignoring the danger, stood up and boldly advanced towards the bathroom. She fired once, hitting the guard in his shoulder. He fired again, this time hitting the bathroom wall. She fired again and struck Pavano's head. He fell forward and Chloe fired again, striking the guard in the chest. Immediately, the house became quiet.

"I had no idea that goddamned arrow was so sharp!" George exclaimed.

"I told you they were hunting arrows," Morgan sniffed. "Now that the danger's over, I'm calling my dad.

Dwight Ingram was standing at the Y's reception desk when Morgan's call came in. "Tell him I've got the cycle and I'm on my way!"

Sensei took an arrow from the quiver and indicated that George should hold his hands up behind him. "Don't move!" he ordered as he prepared to cut the tie. Then he examined the lock on the tie. "This is an old-style one," he said. "I can use a belt buckle's prong to reverse the tie's stopper." He took off his belt and scabbard and inserted the buckle's prong into the tie's knot, forcing back the locking point. Gingerly, he slipped the loops back into their original wide position and freed George's hands.

"Thanks," George said as he winced and rubbed his injured knee.

Beryl looked at Sensei's foot and told Chloe to call 9-1-1. Chloe hesitated. "I'll call the hospital for an ambulance," she said. "The police emergency vehicle is big and won't come up the steep road, but the ambulance will if I tell them to use the station wagon." She made the call and turned to Beryl. "They're leaving now."

Beryl looked at Sensei's foot. "Your sock is stuck to the wound. I don't want to mess with it and get it bleeding again. The ambulance will be here soon. Hang tight." She turned to Chloe. "Let's do a casualty count."

The two women walked through the rooms while being exceptionally careful not to disturb any of the scene. None of the bodies seemed to be showing even a hint of life.

Outside, Dwight Ingram pulled up on the captain's motorcycle and revved the engine a few times before cutting it. He appeared in the front doorway. "What did I miss?"

Beryl went out to greet him. "Not much," she said. "Your intrepid daughter thinks she's indestructible. Fortunately, she's a good shot."

Chloe staggered into his arms. He held her tight, whispering, "It's over now. You're not hurt." He asked, "How's Morgan?"

"He's still in the garage with Mr. Wong," she said.

They went into the garage and looked at the blood-soaked sock. Sensei," he said, "You've lost a lot of blood."

"Type O positive," said Sensei, "in case anyone is interested."

The ambulance came to the third house. Sensei was carried out and put into the vehicle. Morgan climbed into the ambulance. "I'm the property owner," he said to the driver; and then he called to George, "Do you want that knee looked at?"

"No," George said. "I'll take care of it here. You know the routine. Don't make any statements to anyone. Tell them to wait until you're composed to make your statement - an hour or so - or let Sensei do the talking... or us... or invoke your right to counsel. At this point, I don't give a damn what you do. We'll wait here for the police." He turned to Ingram. "I'll call Ross D'Angelo now. I didn't want the ambulance to be interfered with on the road up here, but they're leaving now for the hospital."

Beryl came out of the house and climbed onto the back of the cycle. She called to George, "You can handle things here with Chloe and the cops. I want to be with Sensei." Then she suddenly got off the cycle. She asked Ingram, "Can you take George down to the main house. He's probably better off riding down on your cycle than climbing up into the pickup." They agreed and George got onto the cycle behind Ingram.

George did a mental survey of the third house. "We can leave everything as it is here. We'll just be a couple of houses down the block. They won't want us in there when they process the scene. All those folks are," he took an imaginary roll call, "dead, dead, dead, dead, dead, and dead."

Ingram drove to the main house and helped George to sit comfortably in the kitchen. "Chloe will be right with you," he said. "I'm going back to get Beryl. I guess it's up to you to handle the police. We'll call you from the hospital with an update on Sensei."

Chloe came into the kitchen and sat at the table across from George who got out his phone. "I'm calling Ross D'Angelo," George said. "We're in for a long night of interviews and reports."

Chloe put her hand on his phone. "Wait a bit. Your knee needs some attention and we need to talk." She made an ice pack and placed it against his leg. "Aspirin?" she asked. George grunted. She gave him two aspirin tablets and put pillows under his elevated leg. "Are you hungry?" she asked.

"Sure. You kill a bunch of people and you work up an appetite. Whatcha' got?"

"I can nuke some lasagna."

"Sounds good to me." He called Ross D'Angelo.

"Shots and sutures," Sensei called out to Beryl and Dwight Ingram who stood in the opening of the curtained enclosure. "You missed the great trauma. Tell them," Sensei tapped Morgan's arm with a rolled up medical history page.

"The man of steel is afraid of needles. I'm shocked that he'd mention it. I didn't think anybody would have the guts to own up to the kind of scene he just made." He laughed. "Ten orderlies had to hold him down. Oh, I said we'd go back for the dog. They need to examine it."

Beryl smiled and then pointedly asked Dwight, "Before you go rushing off to pick up the animal, would you mind spelling Morgan? I need to talk to him."

As Morgan and his father changed places, Beryl gently took the younger man's arm. "Let's take a walk."

"I know what you want to discuss," he said defensively. "You're worried about what I am going to tell the police."

Beryl stopped walking and stared at him. "Worried? Not about you or this case. I am worried about George's knee and Sensei's foot. I want to talk to you now out of concern for your father and how your accounts of the evening's events will affect your father - for whom I have great respect. So, right now, I'm going to start by reminding you that I'm not your lawyer or your agent. Don't start confessing to me your part in your mother's death."

"Confessing? Has Chloe been talking?"

"My conversations with Chloe are privileged. I just want to suggest that you talk to Chloe before you talk to anyone else, including your father."

"Why are you concerned about what I say to my father?"

Beryl did not appreciate his tone of voice. "Leave me out of it. When people take a defensive attitude they'll often say or do something that is defiant and reckless. So lose the attitude before you talk yourself into Sing Sing or Attica. Talk to your sister and decide what you are going to reveal about the night of Bill's birthday party. I will not discuss the matter with you. I'm simply asking that you talk it over with Chloe before you start talking to your father about it. Telling him about it will include him in the decision and foist on him the problem of ethics... should you tell the police or should you say nothing? If you wanted to involve him you should have done it before you acted. Why burden him now? Talk to Chloe... discuss the possible consequences with her before you involve anyone else."

"But it's all right for her to involve you?"

"Am I talking to the wallpaper? My conversations with my client are privileged. I'm telling you to talk to your sister before you open your mouth to anyone else. This conversation is over!" She turned around and started to walk back toward the E.R.

"I'm not a stupid man, Miss Tilson. What am I supposed to discuss with her?"

Dwight Ingram had left the Emergency room and was walking down the corridor toward them.

Beryl turned to Morgan and spoke in a low but forceful voice. "Talk to her and you'll figure it out. Don't talk to anyone else until after you've talked to your sister." She called to Dwight, "What's a nice guy like you doin' in a place like this?"

Morgan whispered, "Are you always this tough on your clients?"

"Morgan, you are not my client." She walked ahead to meet Dwight Ingram.

Ross D'Angelo was off duty when George called to tell him the news. "Can you call the station - for protocol's sake - and report the incident to the on-duty captain. He'll dispatch some units immediately. Meanwhile I'll get dressed and be there as soon as possible. 10-4."

As Chloe served dinner, she asked, "So, how did Bill Pavano kill my mother?"

George smiled. "Come on. Cut the baloney. He didn't kill her; and I'd appreciate it if you didn't confess to it. You're a client and privileged confidentiality applies, but I'm not in the mood to test it and too goddamned tired to explain to you what you already know."

"How did whoever killed her do it?"

*"How? Somebody* called her mother and told her to come get her at the bottom of the hill. God knows what she told her to get her away from the party. Then on her side of the road *somebody* set up headlights and battery and remote control beam - or a similar kind of contraption that would blind her temporarily and make her swerve off the road to avoid what she thought was an oncoming car. *Somebody's* brother followed their mother out of the house immediately - he couldn't risk a fiery crash that would draw people before the device could be dismantled and removed."

"You're a professional. How would you rate the scheme on a scale from one to ten?"

"Considering that the killers were amateurs, I'd give it an eight. But that's me. I hate to see a beautiful woman go to waste."

"What did they do or say that gave it away?"

"It was always 'given away.' Beryl had the number before we even took the case. She said that there wasn't a mother in Christendom who could be fooled by an imposter's voice, somebody pretending to be her own kid, especially a kid with whom she was in regular contact."

"Should the person who did this explain things to her father? She knows he'll understand."

"Has she inherited her mother's streak of cruelty? She made her plans without telling her father, but now she wants to dump on him the decision to admit the truth or make him share the guilt of concealing it. If she decides to confess, she should get a lawyer. If she decides to say nothing, she shouldn't burden a third party with the responsibility of having to make that ethical choice. She should talk to her brother and they should consider their next actions from every point of view... all the possible consequences."

"You're right. She needs to talk to her brother. What are you going to do now?"

"Hope my leg gets better. I've got a long drive home."

"You're not gonna tell anyone?"

"No! I can't prove anything. I have zero evidence. Ross D'Angelo has an interesting theory. Let him work it out... or not. As far as I'm concerned, the birthday party accident and tonight's activities are two different matters. I bear witness only to tonight's events."

"What should I tell them about tonight?"

"The truth! The truth about actions, not thoughts. And don't try to tell anybody else's version of the truth."

Chloe's eyes widened. Her chin quivered and she shook her head. "How can I do that? Should I get a lawyer to talk for me?"

George spoke gruffly. "*Now* you consider the law? Jesus, Chloe! Stop acting like a helpless child." He rubbed his knee.

Chloe began to whine. "I don't know what to tell them."

"That's what happens when you take the law into your own hands. Before you do it, you're so sure of the guilt or innocence of everyone who'll be touched by your actions. Afterwards you're not so sure. And then you're so obsessed with justifying what you've done that you can't be rational and objective. It's all so much bullshit drama!"

"Tell me what you mean! Actions, not thoughts?"

"First, recognize the difference between what you know is true, and what you've been told is true, and what you guess is true. Here's the truth. Listen. See if you can understand the proper way to tell your story.

"Last Monday, in Philadelphia, you were taken by your Aunt Marietta to the offices of George Wagner and Beryl Tilson, private investigators, and their associate Sensei Percy Wong. Your Aunt had made the appointment. You were having trouble accepting your mother's death and you wanted to rule out the possibility that Bill Pavano killed your mother. So you engaged the investigators to find proof, if there were any, that he was responsible for her death. If they want to know why your Aunt picked my firm, tell them to ask her.

"In the course of that investigation, Miss Tilson wanted to interview Wes Richter and asked you to accompany her. If they ask you why Beryl wanted to speak to Wes, tell them to ask her.

"You and Beryl went to Vermont to interview Mr. Pavano's close friend Wes Richter. When you arrived at his residence, the police were there and *you were told* that Mr. Richter had been shot and killed, in an 'execution style' murder. Do you get this? You didn't 'discover' that Richter was murdered, you were 'told' that he was. You could have been told a lie. You don't know, so don't speculate or give credence to what you don't know. Do you understand the difference between saying you discovered and saying you were told?"

"Yes, I get it. If I say I discovered that he was dead, I'm vouching for his death."

"You returned from Vermont. Miss Tilson expressed her fear of Mr. Pavano's associates, Mr. Cardinale and his three bodyguards. You and she blundered into a siege in the so-called "third" house on the hilltop. You saw a dead man on the living room floor, and you heard screams coming from the bathroom, and you saw the back of Mr. Cardinale standing in the bathroom doorway. *You were later told* that the dead man on the floor was the first of Cardinale's three bodyguards, and that he had been shot in an exchange of gunfire with Mr. Wagner, and you were also told that that Mr. Pavano was being tortured in the bathroom by Mr. Cardinale and another of the bodyguards. If they ask how he was being tortured, tell them you did not witness anything and cannot answer the question.

"The interior door to the garage was open and you and Miss Tilson looked inside and saw that Mr. Wong, Mr. Wagner, and your brother were bound prisoners of the second of Mr. Cardinale's bodyguards. There was a great deal of blood on the floor which had come from Mr.Wong's foot. *You later were told* that he had been bitten by Mr. Cardinale's dog.

"In an attempt to rescue the prisoners, Miss Tilson shot the second bodyguard in the garage, whereupon Mr. Cardinale turned and shot once at you and Miss Tilson. Miss Tilson returned fire and shot Mr. Cardinale who collapsed on the floor. *You later were told* that he had in his possession the first bodyguard's gun which he had picked up from the living room floor.

"Miss Danvers, your housekeeper, suddenly attacked Miss Tilson with a broom handle. She knocked the Beretta from Miss Tilson's hand. You saw that Danvers was attempting to get the gun and you dove for it and succeeded in grasping it. Danvers tried to get the gun away from you, and in the skirmish, you shot her.

"The third bodyguard in the bathroom, who was covered in Mr. Cardinale's spurting blood, began to shoot at you and you shot back. Your shots hit him and probably Mr. Pavano, too. His shots missed you. You cannot say with any certainty how many bullets you fired.

"Is this an accurate account? Or, do you know something I don't know?"

Chloe seemed astonished to hear a straightforward account of the incident. "That's what happened. Why does it seem so simple?"

"Because I drained the emotion out of it. When you leave out egotistic justifications and excuses and reasons and suspicions, you get down to an unvarnished account. Just tell the truth and don't let anybody goad you into getting emotional or into telling anybody else's truth. Learn to say, 'I don't know. You'll have to ask someone else.'"

"What should I tell them about Morgan?"

"Nothing! Didn't I just tell you to confine your account to your own actions and the actions of your agents. Morgan can speak for himself. Don't even mention his name. If they press you - and I can't imagine that they will - invoke your right to speak to an attorney."

"I'm sorry. I'm just so overwhelmed by everything that happened. You're used to shooting people. I'm not."

"Chloe, in all my years as a cop, I never planned to execute anybody. Just tell the truth about what happened tonight without trying to make yourself Joan of Arc."

"You don't have to be so mean."

"I'm not being mean by telling you to drain the emotion out of your account. Don't discuss thoughts and suppositions and other people's assertions and intentions."

"What truth should I tell them if they ask about my mother's death?"

"Get a lawyer and he'll tell you to say that on advice of counsel you may not discuss the business interests of your mother, your step-father, or your Sicilian guests, or her death. Get this through your head right now... there will be investigations into your aunt's 'Home for Unwed Mothers' and Wes and Shira Lodge and Shivadas Herbal products plus a host of things I don't know anything about. Your mother was not a nice person and her life is going to be laid bare. Who killed her may be much less important than the fact that she and her criminal allies are dead. Don't be surprised if the yacht is seized. And the Home in Maine, too. You'll be lucky if Ingram House stays with you and Morgan and your father. Maybe you can pool your resources and buy it back from the government if it's ever seized. Just don't contribute to the case against your family by opening your mouths gratuitously. Get a lawyer. He'll tell you what I'm telling you. Limit your remarks to the matter that is being investigated: that is the events of Friday, October 28th. Talk to your brother first and decide on which course you want to follow. And then get counsel."

"All right. I get it!"

She began to clear away the dinner dishes. "I have to stay positive. I can't believe that after all these years, my father will be home here, in his house, with us. It will be like we've moved into a new house."

"If my leg doesn't start feeling better, I may be your first houseguest. Ok. Before the thundering herd arrives, tell me what motivated you? Incidentally, we know about the Hawaiian burn lies. Nice story, though."

Chloe was surprised. "You investigated me?"

"What did you think? That we'd encounter crime of this magnitude and not check anything? Was anything you told us true? I'd like that story about Bill telling the priest that he didn't know where Bill was to be true. If you made it up, don't tell me."

"The truth all came out... finally. That was true and so was the Harem dress."

"May I say that with the exception of your father, your family is the most accomplished bunch of liars I've ever encountered. You, Morgan, your aunt, your mother. Have any of you ever told the truth about anything?"

"What did Sensei learn about my Aunt's involvement?"

"Not much beyond that she's not running a home for unwed mothers. It's not even a Catholic institution. It probably functions as a place that treats religious personnel with emotional problems. Possibly a few secret guests hide out there whenever things get too hot for them elsewhere. They probably pay big bucks for the service." He slapped the table. "Now, what happened this summer? And tell me the truth!"

Chloe stood up and walked to the doorway. She leaned against the jamb and tried to speak casually. "In Hawaii, Doctor Boorman had recognized a "Shivadas" sticker on my suitcase. He said something to a student who said something to somebody else and when it got back to me, I had to act on it."

"I know," George acknowledged the story. "He told a UN executive about it. I also know about the enormous salaries your mother's charities paid her and Bill and Mr. Cardinale, too. More than 92% of what she received in donations for the refugees went into their pockets."

Chloe shook her head and began to speak softly and without emotion. "And 92% wasn't enough. The other eight percent went to purchasing phony medicines. When I found out what she was doing with those fake medicines, I told Morgan. He had suspected it all along. He met me in Brazzaville, in the Congo... last July... so hot! We went to a camp and pretended to be casual observers. We talked to a medic. He knew all about the worthless medicines and was happy to talk about the problem. In his office he had pictures of victims and a few of the people who may have been the swindlers. He mentioned Shivadas. He was a Hindu and it offended him profoundly that his Lord's name had been used by evil people for such an evil purpose.

"We were resigned to seeing her face. There were others, too. But he pointed to a shot of my mother, smiling at a baby, getting her photograph taken with it. He said he later heard 'this woman' laughing in a restaurant. She was having such a good time even after seeing all that horror. I knew what she was capable of. She's the one who forced me to have the abortion, not Bill. Bill may have been worried about Sicily, but she was worried about her business. She didn't want a scandal's negative publicity. My mother was all about money. I think the only man she ever had any feelings for was Mr. Cardinale. He worshipped her. I felt sorry for myself for what she had done to Danny and me and our baby. And then I saw those people. They were so hungry and sick. What did I have to complain about?

"People always have theories about family life when a kid goes bad. They either feel sorry for the parents or they blame them. They're full of advice about child-rearing. But nobody has anything to say when a parent goes bad. The kids bear the shame and the punishments. And they can't even use the excuse that their parents fell in with a bad crowd!

"How can people, who have experienced life and know what hardship is, victimize people who are already suffering so much?"

George tried to help her to understand. "Human nature has a dark side. You see it in the *cause* of the refugee problem. You see it in the result. Thousands of refugees escape their own country and come as an invasion to a neighboring country. Some host countries are poor and don't want the refugees draining their limited resources, bringing crime and disease, and so on. They resent the refugees. They think, 'Ah, they couldn't govern themselves *there* and now they come *here* and try to destroy our way of life.' So they're happy to buy bad drugs for them. The bad drugs cost pennies to produce but institutions pay top dollar for them. The profit gets split between the manufacturers, purveyors, and the purchasing agents of the host countries. The refugees suffer and die. Everybody else likes the system."

"That might explain the reasons why people purchase the bad medicines, but how does it explain my mother's reason for producing and selling them?"

"It doesn't. She was just plain evil! I thought you knew that," he grinned. He checked his watch and called Ted Cardone in Philadelphia. He put the call on speaker and told Chloe to listen carefully to the conversation. Exactly as he had wanted her to tell the story, he repeated it to Cardone.

"Jesus!" Cardone finally said, "You've had a busy night. I hope your man recovers. Any conclusions about Catherine Pavano's death?"

"Ted, the 'suspect pool' is pretty murky right now. Nobody's been charged, but Captain Ross D'Angelo of the local police force has a good theory about the means by which the victim's car was forced off the road." He saw a car pull into the parking lot. "That's probably Ross D'Angelo pulling into the driveway here. You can contact him for any additional information. Ross also has photographs of the birthday party held the night of the accident. There are many interesting guests in the pictures, including Cardinale. You might want to ask him to send you copies. If you don't want to let him into the loop, I can probably get a set of prints from Dr. Ingram - the man who took them. Ok. Gotta go. 10-4." He disconnected the call and turned to Chloe. "Are you ready?"

Chloe began to cry. She sat down and covered her face with her hands.

"Remember!" George mussed her hair, "Tell the truth. Tell them exactly what happened tonight. You don't know why anything happened. No theories. No opinions. Separate what you know from what you were told and from what you surmise. Ballistics will fill in all the blanks, as we say."

Ross D'Angelo was at the door.